ALLEN COUNTY PUBLIC LIBRARY

3 1833 00721 ☑ S0-BXL-270

GUN BLAST

Tom Slattery didn't want to wear a badge, but when Sheriff Wright was bushwhacked by an unknown gunman, no one else dared to take over the job. Slattery was well aware that Yellowstone City lay squarely under the thumb of Byron Kenneally, who owned the biggest spread in Montana Territory, and Slattery aimed to prove that no one, not even Kenneally, was above the law.

GUN BLAST

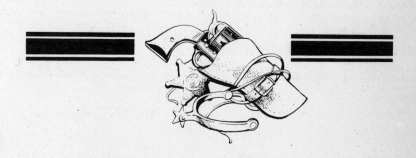

Steven C. Lawrence

ATLANTIC LARGE PRINT
Chivers Press, Bath, England.
John Curley & Associates Inc.,
South Yarmouth, Mass., USA.

Library of Congress Cataloging in Publication Data

Lawrence, Steven C.
  Gun blast.

  "Atlantic large print"
  1. Large type books.   I. Title.
  [PS3562.A916G8   1985]   813'.54   84–14918
  ISBN 0–89340–804–2

British Library Cataloguing in Publication Data

Lawrence, Steven C.
  Gun blast.—Large print ed.—(Atlantic
  large print)
  I. Title
  813'.54[F]   PS3562.A916

  ISBN 0–85119–696–9

This Large Print edition is published by Chivers Press, England, and
John Curley & Associates, Inc, U.S.A. 1985

Published by arrangement with Dorchester Publishing Co, Inc

U.K. Hardback ISBN 0 85119 696 9
U.S.A. Softback ISBN 0 89340 804 2

Copyright © MCMLXXVII by Tower Publications, Inc
All rights reserved

Allen County Public Library
Ft. Wayne, Indiana

2247296

CHAPTER ONE

The stagecoach, an Abbot-Downing Concord fresh out of the line shop after a week of greasing, reconditioning and repainting for this first run into northern Montana, rolled just fast enough to keep ahead of the dust the wheels threw back onto the endless stretch of tall grass. The scrollwork lettered along the panel below the luggage deck, *Bismarck—Casper—Helena Stage Company*, reflected golden yellow in the mid-morning sunshine. The driver was a whiskered, old hand at his job. He held the reins easily, feeling the gentle rock and sway of the coach on its thoroughbraces. It had been a good run, safe, with no problems, not even any gripes from the ten men who were passengers on the coach seats.

Alongside him the shotgun rider leaned forward to see beyond the screening timber that lined the river and blocked his view of the town ahead.

'Yellowstone City,' he remarked. 'All I c'n make out is 'leven, twelve buildin's, besides the houses. Not much of a place to be addin' as a regular stop.'

'It's growin', Billy.' Len Morgan waved one hand across the sweep of grass toward the distant, sheltering windbreaks of the Madison and Gallatin Mountains. 'You see the grass, and cattle. More people'll be comin' in. It'll be growin'.'

Billy Patten watched the rutted road. He knew better than to argue with old Morgan. He'd had a full view of this Calligan Valley when they'd broken from the thick timber of the southern pass. He'd grown up on a ranch himself and knew the value of the long, unbroken miles of virgin rangeland, brownish-green with the grass watered by the lazy course of the Calligan River flowing down from the northern mountains. Yet it seemed so isolated, this valley, miles from their final stop at the capital in Helena.

'I don't know,' Billy said shortly. 'I'd think the line'd have a straighter route goin' through Bozeman.'

'They would, if the owners only thought of right now,' the old man told him. 'There's talk of petitionin' for statehood. And of buildin' the Northern Pacific straight through this valley. The man who's bein' talked up as becomin' first senator

2

from the state in Washington...'

'Watch it!'

Billy had shouted the words. The double-barreled Greener he'd laid flat across his thighs because of the peace and quiet came up in both of his hands. He aimed at the buckboard that had seemed to appear out of nowhere, rolling straight at them from the higher grass to their left, bearing down on them.

Morgan yanked back on the reins and grabbed for the brake. One of the passengers yelled, 'What's happening? Are they going to hold us up?'

'No. They wouldn't try so close to town!' another answered. 'They wouldn't dare!'

'They're tryin' to run us off the road!'

The stagecoach's six team horses were stopping. Grating squeals of straining brake blocks cut through the heat of the air. Billy Patten held the Greener steady, both barrels centered on the buckboard's driver. Meadow larks flushed by the bouncing, jouncing wagon flew straight into the sky. More birds rose, chattering, flapping in every direction to escape the hoofs of the lively black stallion whipped ahead by the driver and the churning wheels throwing up clods of dirt and thick

3

clouds of dust over the grass.

'Don't shoot!' one of the passengers called. 'It's Neddy Kenneally! He's only funnin'! Don't shoot!'

The buckboard driver was young, eighteen or nineteen, the same age as the youngest stage passenger who'd called out. Billy Patten kept his shotgun aimed. The young driver slashed his silver-ferruled whip across his horse's spine. He was laughing, and the boy alongside him on the wagon seat laughed as the buckboard came speeding through the grass straight at the stage horses.

Len Morgan swore. He stood up from the seat and strained to hold the terrified team. Whinnying, kicking, banging rumps, flanks and hoofs against each other, the trapped animals shook the stage. Billy Patten was almost thrown from the box. While the horse and wagon drove past the coach, barely missing the team, he lowered the shotgun and reached to grip tight to the seat. A hawk rose into the sky beyond the buckboard. The large bird made a wide curve through the blue while the buckboard driver swung the wagon and again headed toward the stage.

'You keep off!' Morgan bellowed. 'Don't

you come near us again!'

'Don't!' Billy added. He motioned with the Greener. 'Dammit, don't you try to do it!'

The driver pulled the buckboard in alongside the coach. Laughing loudly, he waved the whip at Morgan. 'Come on, we'll race you into town!'

'Not on your life!' He had the team quiet. 'You could've hurt my horses!'

'I'd've paid for it!' He was tall and handsome, his dark-tanned face grinning from under his sombrero. 'You afraid to race!'

'I'm not a damn fool!' Morgan eased himself back onto the seat. He wiped the sleeve of his shirt across his sweating forehead. 'I'm reportin' this to the town marshal!'

'You're lucky I didn't blow your head off!' Billy Patten said. 'Stupid fool trick like that!'

The buckboard driver's smile vanished. His eyes flicked to the passengers. He nodded to the youngest who had called to Billy. 'Good to see you, Eddie Jones.' His stare, hard and tight, returned to Patten. 'Watch who you call stupid.'

'You wise-mouthed bastard!' Billy

Patten said. 'You were a little older, I'd thrash you for that!'

The driver looked Patten up and down. Then he looked at Len Morgan. 'You haven't got the guts to race. I'm wasting my time.'

He shook the reins and started the wagon ahead, onto the deep-rutted roadway toward the town.

Morgan hesitated before he released the brake. He hung his head down over the box to see into the coach. 'Anyone hurt?' he questioned.

He was answered with a chorus of, 'No. No, I'm all right. We're all right.'

Eddie Jones called to Patten. 'You better watch it. Neddy Kenneally ain't the one to call stupid. Or a wise-mouth bastard.'

Patten did not answer. He laid the Greener flat across his thighs. He wiped both hands on his jeans, drying the sweat of his palms. A loud painful screech made him glance into the sky. The hawk had dived on one of the birds. Having made its kill, the attacker swept down, still clutching its victim, toward the thickness of the screening timber along the river bend.

'Watch that Kenneally,' Len Morgan said to Billy quietly. 'Stay close while we change teams.'

Patten looked at him. 'I'm not runnin' from any wise kid, Len.'

'He just ain't any wise kid! That man I said was the one they're talkin' up for senator.' He nodded toward the eastern end of the valley. 'That's the Kenneally kid's uncle.' He nodded again to Billy Patten. 'I'm tellin' you. Be careful.'

★   ★   ★

'Careful,' Tom Slattery said to his wife.

He had swung down from the seat of their buckboard and had tied their gray mare to the hitchrail in front of Blumberg's General Store before he reached up to help Judy off the step plate. 'Move slow, and careful,' he repeated.

The front of her blue cotton dress had started to show her condition in the four weeks since they had been in town to do their monthly shopping. The gabbers of Yellowstone City wouldn't miss it, and they'd have something else to gossip about now. He and Judy had laughed, talking about that riding in, guessing who'd notice first, and the reactions they'd get. But he was past due for his first child at thirty-five,

7

with their own home and land, and so much to offer their children.

Judy took his hand. Then she paused, her head held high as though she read the poster nailed to the store's false front announcing the town's Jubilee Days. But she wasn't reading, she listened. They both stared westward toward the sharp, quick clopping of a horse's hoofs and the noise of a jouncing wagon.

The Kenneally buckboard had rumbled across the Calligan's thick log bridge and was speeding into Centre Street. Judy's face tightened, and her fingers tightened on her husband's hand. She continued to pause.

'Step off slow,' he told her. 'I'll go inside with you and see if Myron has that bolt of cloth you ordered.'

She smiled, her hand still gripped tight while she stepped down. He felt a need to put his arms around her and hold her. She'd been so careful since the first moment she'd known she carried their baby. He'd known her through the hard time of a trail drive a thousand miles north from Texas, and through man-made troubles, and injury and illness, and the drought of burning summer heat and the freeze of winter cold and snow and ice storms. She showed more worry now, and he was constantly amazed that this woman he had loved from first sight could be so strong and yet so girllike, and make him even more want to hold her and touch the softness of her dark hair.

The store's screen door swung open above them, the sound barely audible below the noise of the Kenneally horse and wagon. Myron Blumberg stepped onto the porch. The small, thin storekeeper stared toward the street, his mouth bitten into a straight line. Then he looked at the Slatterys.

'That family,' he said. 'They ought to be held down.' His eyes softened, brightened. He grinned widely and held out both hands to Judy. 'Well, it's good to see you. All of you.'

Judy smiled, and Slattery laughed. She moved faster, up the stairs, into the store. Myron offered his hand to Slattery, and shook it briskly.

The store was a long, wide room with a door at the rear leading into a storeroom, and beyond a huge wood stove, a staircase to Blumberg's living quarters on the second floor. Slattery trailed his wife down the

9

center aisle past shelves and counters filled with boots, shoes, pants, shirts, underwear, stockings, fresh bolts of dry goods, bright prints and calicoes, all the products which showed the storekeeper's thriving business.

'You'll be needing more cloth,' Blumberg said to Judy. 'I'll have Tom carry out what I've put up for you.' He pointed to a wooden box on the counter near the coffee grinder. 'And you can start filling another box.'

'We can't take too much now,' Slattery began. 'I'll know better after we make the drive to Billings next month.'

'I didn't ask you that,' Blumberg said.

'But we can't.'

'You didn't ask anything of anyone in this valley when a man like Ralph Goodlove tried to take everything from us.' He was silent, listening. Through the long front window they could see the Abbot-Downing Concord stagecoach roll past toward the stage office. Blumberg nodded. 'It's an important day for all of us, Tom.' He smiled at Judy. 'You pick what you want.'

Slattery lifted the box. It was heavier than he had judged. Myron had added some canned goods under the cloth.

He hefted the box going down the aisle, balancing it on his left shoulder. He hadn't forgotten the trouble of almost three years ago, when he and men like Steve Murfee and Mal Weaver had stopped Goodlove's attempt to take every acre of the valley. But he couldn't live on that, letting Myron stretch his credit even for what he and Judy, and the baby, needed. The trail drive he and the other ranchers would make in September to market their cattle would bring in enough to carry through the next year. That's all he could plan on.

He pushed the screen door open, realizing he'd by habit kept his right hand and side free. He wore no gun, hadn't had to since he'd been married and settled on his own homestead. He had taken along his Winchester carbine, slid under the seat of the buckboard, only to be ready if a snake or mountain lion or bear threatened.

He'd felt even more settled since the morning three months ago Judy had told him she was sure of the baby. He and Judy wanted the baby, had hoped and prayed for it, and the promise of their life in Calligan Valley. He loved the wide fertile Montana land and the high sky over the Madisons and Gallatins and the color of the grass and

11

the river that was wider than a hundred yards in so many spots and so deep and good for swimming and where he and his unborn sons, and daughters, could spend so many hours fishing for bullheads and catfish . . .

The voices, men arguing, yelling, bounced across Centre onto the store porch. The Concord stage was pulled up at the doorway of the jail. The Kenneally buckboard was stopped near the walk. The shouting was between the stage driver and his shotgun rider, and two of the Kenneally boys.

Slattery put the box into the wagon and crossed the street.

'You tried to run us down!' the shotgun rider was accusing, shouting into Neddy Kenneally's face. 'I think you oughta be taken in for it!'

'Aw, hell,' Neddy snapped back, 'we were only looking for a race.' He waved the whip he held in a circular motion to include the town, the entire valley. 'You have to learn how it is around here.'

'I learned all I have to!' Patten had shoved his sweatstained hat back on his hair, showing the full length of his flushed, angry face. He stared around at the

12

passengers who were being crowded in closer and closer by the town men attracted by the yelling. 'You know how scared you were!' Then, his stare flicked from the whiskered driver to Albert Wright who had come onto the boardwalk from the jail office. 'Morgan'll tell you, Deputy! He knows what could've happened as well as me!'

'Aw, hell,' Neddy Kenneally said again. 'You aren't going to take us in for that, Al?'

'Ask the passengers!' the shotgun rider snapped. 'You know what c'n happen from drivin' so fast!'

'I thought we were going to be run down!' one of the passengers said. 'They could've knocked us over!'

'I did too!' another added. 'They can't be allowed to run loose like that!'

'Aw, hell.' Neddy looked at the rider who had been on the wagon seat beside him. 'We was only funnin', Jim.'

Jim Kenneally nodded. He was almost as tall as his cousin's six-feet-two, his features as dark-tanned and good-looking under his sombrero. 'Al, you know us.'

The deputy scanned the faces in the crowd. He was older than the Kenneallys, in his mid-twenties, as tall as Neddy. 'You

13

don't have the right to run a stage off the road,' he said.

'We didn't run it off the road.' Neddy glanced around. His eyes flicked past Slattery, who had been pressed in near him by those joining at the rear of the crowd. Neddy motioned with his whip to the youngest passenger on the stage. 'Eddie, you didn't think we were running you off the road, did you?'

Jim Kenneally added before Eddie Jones could answer, 'You didn't, Eddie. Did you?'

Eddie Jones shook his head. 'I yelled up to the driver,' he answered. He grinned at Neddy and Jim. 'I told him you was only funnin'.' He grinned at the other passengers close to him and nodded to them. 'Didn't I tell the driver? I did, didn't I?'

'Yes,' one of the men said. 'I heard you holler to him.'

Len Morgan said, 'He did call up to me. I jest wanted to report...'

'No!' Billy Patten cut in. 'I could've shot him! Both of them! I had reason to! He's gotta learn what he can cause!'

'You big-mouth bastard!' Neddy Kenneally snarled. 'You just want blood!'

14

He spit in the shotgun rider's face. 'I'll give you reason!'

Patten bellowed an oath. The shocked onlookers edged back as the shotgun rider wiped spittle from his eyes. Neddy Kenneally raised the whip to slash at Patten. Slattery reached out and grabbed the raised hand to stop him. Then, Patten's doubled fist smashed Neddy flush on the mouth.

One of Neddy's teeth flew out. Blood gushed from his torn lips. He went down to his knees and stayed there kneeling in the dust blubbering obscene curses.

The deputy moved in between Patten and Neddy. 'Come with me,' he told the shotgun rider.

'What!' Patten pointed to Neddy, both of his hands gripping his bleeding mouth while he pushed himself to his feet. 'He started it!'

'And you, too,' the deputy told Neddy. 'We'll settle this inside.'

Neddy wavered on his bootheels. He lowered his left hand and stared at the blood.

'Sonovabitch,' he mumbled, pressing the swollen lips. His stare was a glare of hate, for the shotgun rider, and for Slattery.

'You sonsabitches,' he said, the words clear and distinct. 'You'll pay for this!' He looked at his cousin. 'Go out to The Village, Jim. Tell Uncle.' The hate-filled eyes switched back again. His voice was quieter, deadly certain.

'You'll pay! You damn well will pay!'

CHAPTER TWO

Sid Rooney was the first to come. That same evening, just before sunset.

Slattery had not told Judy of the threat. He hadn't wanted to worry her, and partially because the threat had been made by the anger of a hurt boy not yet grown into a man.

And because Judy was too happy, chattering all during the ten-mile drive back to their home about how the town women had been happy to know of the baby, and the advice they had given, and of Nancy Weaver's almost having had words with Susan Huffaker about who could come and stay in the house when her time came. Doctor Hobson was a fine doctor, they'd said, but he was still young, without

16

a wife of his own, and a woman, women, would be of more help.

Judy had kept up talking even during their evening meal. He'd smiled as he'd left her to walk out along the river, as he did each night. It was the time of day she had grown to understand he needed by himself, after he cared for his own black stallion in the barn, and the team horses, when he looked over the acres of wheat and potatoes and varied vegetables they had planted, and checked their eight-three head of cattle.

The deep red of sunset started to fade by the time he reached the river bank. The whole rim of the southern mountains, the peaks still spotted white here and there with snow above the timber line, gradually lost the soft pink color, and he stood in the trees along the Calligan's high north bank watching the darkness of the valley floor thicken to rise up and up and become thicker and thicker until the peaks blended with the sky and all seemed to become one widening patch of gray which sparkled with pinpoints of stars.

He had stood so many nights with Judy and watched, together. The past two weeks she had become tired earlier and needed her rest. They'd have so many, many

17

evenings ahead, he thought, with their son, with their sons and daughters . . .

Slattery turned quickly when he heard the horse.

He was surprised the rider had come the three-hundred feet from the house without his hearing. He had been so intent in thought.

He smiled when he saw it was Sid Rooney.

But Rooney did not smile.

Rooney was the Kenneally ranch foreman. He took charge of everything in what was called The Village at the eastern edge of the valley: two ranches, actually, for Byron Kenneally cared for the family of his dead brother, as well as his own wife and four children. Rooney was thin and wiry, close to sixty years, but he could ride, rope, brand and do any ranch work as well as the Kenneallys' youngest hand. He sat his saddle erect, his head back, with the sureness and pride of his position.

He reined in close to Slattery, so despite the deepening dark each man could see the other's face.

'You roughed up one of the boys, Slattery,' Rooney said. 'He's being held.'

'I tried to stop a fight, Sid.'

18

'You roughed him up.' He leaned forward now, looking straight down into Slattery's eyes. 'Mister Byron is sendin' for a circuit judge.'

'It wasn't that important, Sid.'

Rooney didn't seem to hear. 'You know Mister Byron's plans for this valley. What he wants for himself, and the family. It has to be clear cut the boys were doin' no wrong, so there won't be talk later on. We'll let you know when to appear in town.'

Slattery watched Rooney's eyes, and he felt a tightening in his chest.

'Did you come by my house?' he asked.

'I spoke to your missus.'

Slattery moved closer to Rooney, looking him straight in the eyes. 'I'll go into town and appear when I should. Al Wright will tell me.' Rooney's lips parted, but Slattery spoke first, adding, 'You don't come to my house. You or anyone from The Village, until this is settled. No one talks to my wife.'

Rooney simply stared at him. Slattery began to walk from the trees. He half-turned when Rooney's hard, cold words followed him through the dark.

'The boy's goin' to be missin' three

teeth. The one who did it's still in that jail.'

Slattery continued walking, wanting to see and talk to his wife.

*　　*　　*

'No, he was very nice,' Judy said. 'He left his horse near the well and knocked on the door and asked for you.'

Slattery nodded. He started a yawn to let her see he was tired.

'Why, Tom?' Judy watched him. 'Did he say anything to you that worries you?'

'Only that I have to appear at the hearing, or whatever the circuit judge decides. The other men who were there will appear, too.' He shook his head, and yawned again. 'It's very important to Kenneally that no one criticize his family. He has his plans to be the state's first senator.'

She nodded, and he believed she would go into the bedroom to get ready for bed.

Her eyes widened. She placed both of her hands on her belly, holding herself at her sudden thought.

'Those boys were driving so fast when they came into town.' She spoke softly, her face tightening as it had when she had paused before she had stepped down off their buckboard, her hand firm in his. 'I hate to think of what would happen if we were driven off the road.'

Slattery didn't answer. He began to unbutton his shirt while his wife went into the bedroom. He waited until she was in bed before he made a double check of the window locks and the locked front door and the lock on the rear kitchen door.

Rooney's riding almost twenty miles just to speak with him meant more than it seemed at first. He'd stay calm, would act natural, but he could not push from his mind the hard, cold sound of Rooney's voice, nor could he hold back the tight little fist of worry that was squeezing him inside his chest.

CHAPTER THREE

The town men came early the next morning.

Slattery was up and out before five, running through the drizzle that held on after a midnight rain, going into the small barn to tend the horses and milk cow as

21

usual. He finished breakfast, sat and talked with Judy the extra ten to fifteen minutes he usually stayed in their kitchen until she began to clean the table saying if he intended to clear river brush to add graze land to the east meadow, she would bring out his lunch in the wicker basket, and they could sit under the trees on the banking and have one of their picnics.

He drove off in the buckboard satisfied everything was to Judy as it usually was. She hadn't mentioned Sid Rooney, or the trouble in Yellowstone City. She had spoken of Ellen Shields, saying she might drive over and visit today. Their nearest neighbors to the west, Ellen and Frank Shields visited often with their two little children. It would be a normal day.

He hadn't made anything special of sliding the Winchester carbine under the wagon seat. But he wanted the weapon with him. He didn't know what Byron Kenneally was capable of. The man had such a drive to get ahead and become a power in the valley. Slattery had sensed that when the Kenneally families had come in to settle longer than two years ago.

And Rooney had been so cold and matter-of-fact, warning him, in his way.

The thick river brush was wet. He was sprayed with water off the cottonwoods, willows, and elders while he chopped at tangled vines and dug to be able to pull up roots. The sky had stayed cloudy, the morning gray and chill with a steady damp breeze. The clouds held no more rain, were more of an overhang of thin, misty fog that shifted and drifted visibly, the haze so low over the grassy flat its tenuous gray obscured the sun yet did not lessen its heat.

Slattery saw the surrey and horse and rider when they were still far off.

He had been pulling at a particularly stubborn root, sweating along his shoulders and spine. He'd straightened to pick up his shovel. As he often had during the hour he worked, he glanced eastward.

He could see four or five miles, further when the haze reluctantly thinned and for a few minutes opened on shallow patches of sunshine. The faint rise and fall of the tall grass was deceptive, brownish-gray, some stretches shining wet and green.

Beyond one long stretch of green, the top of the surrey was visible. He knew whose vehicle it was.

Irving Rinehart owned the New Yellowstone Hotel and Yellowstone

Saloon. A heavy-set man in his early sixties, he had campaigned and been defeated for Town Council in the spring election. The defeat did not stop him from attending each Council meeting and volunteering for committee work which helped the town's progress. Clifton Howard, riding alongside the surrey, ran the livery stable. A thin man, twenty years younger than Rinehart, Howard was no less energetic in his efforts to help the town grow and prosper.

Rinehart turned off the valley road and raised his left hand in a friendly gesture before he reached Slattery. The surrey, drawn by a pair of perfectly matched bays, was as expensive and finely built as the vehicles Byron Kenneally used to bring his wife and family into Yellowstone City. Slattery's stockman's eye judged the black stallion Howard rode as one of the finest bred horses he had ever seen.

'Tom,' Rinehart said in his soft Alabama drawl. 'Good to see you.' His round face turned left and right, studying the land and grass. 'You've done a great deal of work since I stopped in before the election. A great deal.'

'Yes,' Howard agreed. 'You've got the best spread this side of town.'

'You want to stop in the house?' Slattery offered. 'My wife will be glad to have you visit.'

Rinehart shook his head. 'We're here because of the trouble yesterday. You were one of the men who saw what happened.'

'I was.'

'A circuit judge will be here from Bozeman this afternoon. He's going to hold a hearing.'

'I'll be there. But I can't see why a judge had to be called in, all the way from Bozeman.'

Rinehart nodded. 'It's necessary, though. You know how people talk. I don't blame Byron for wanting to have the misunderstanding straightened out once and for all.'

'Ned spit in a man's face, Mr. Rinehart. That's more than a misunderstanding.'

Clifton Howard said, 'Well, he was provoked. You know Ned's spirited, and he's got a temper.'

'From the stage driver's story,' Slattery said, 'Ned and Jim Kenneally did the provoking.'

'It's only their word against the Kenneally boys,' Rinehart answered gently but firmly. 'They were cursed out by the shotgun rider. Tom, you know how stage men are. A rough lot.'

'I know Jimmy Kenneally was held in jail last summer for beating up the Loomis boy. He was drunk, and his uncle saw to it then that it was cleared up.'

Rinehart shook his head. 'A boy's fight. If Murfee hadn't been so quick to act—'

'Steve Murfee was a good sheriff, a friend of mine. He kept a strong law.'

Rinehart again shook his head. 'That has nothing to do with this, Tom. We were asked to inform you of the hearing. And to ask you to be ready to state what you witnessed.'

Slattery nodded. 'The deputy sent you out.'

'Well, not the deputy,' Howard began.

'We're here because of Byron Kenneally,' Rinehart said. 'Look, Tom. He has to have this whole ridiculous affair ended. You can't blame him. You just say what the others are going to say. That the boy was provoked.'

'And whitewash Ned? I didn't see it that way.'

Howard leaned over the saddle horn to speak, but Rinehart waved him silent.

'Look,' Rinehart said, the softness gone

26

from his drawl and his fleshy jowls flushing. 'Byron has plans for our town. He's worked hard to build up his own land. He has influence with the railroad people back east.' He swung his hand in a quick motion that took in the entire valley. His eyes shifted from Slattery toward the house. Slattery looked around and saw Judy stood in the front doorway, watching them. 'You know what a railroad would mean to us,' he heard Rinehart continue. 'Even the stage line. Byron got that for us, and this first stage has had to stay over a few days so this can be settled. It's all got to be settled. Tom, you know the plans that have been made to celebrate the town's anniversary the end of this week.'

Slattery and Judy intended to go in only on the last day of the jubilee. They had too much to do here. Now another day would be spent away from their ranch. 'I'll be in,' he said.

'Dammit,' Howard began, sitting stiff-backed. 'They have Eddie Jones' testimony. He was on the stage.'

'I'll be in,' Slattery repeated.

Silence fell, a taut, heavy silence. Rinehart glanced toward the house. He raised his left hand and waved to Judy, who returned the wave. Howard swung his stallion. Rinehart started the team of matched bay horses, the iron rims of the wheels cutting deep into the damp earth.

Slattery looked toward his wife. Judy had not moved. She watched the surrey and the rider angle through the grass toward the valley road.

Slattery put the ax, pick, and shovel into the buckboard and began to hitch the team horse. His irritation had grown to anger now, at Rooney for warning him and at the two town men who had made it so clear exactly what was expected of him.

★   ★   ★

'They're holding the hearing today so it will be straightened out before the celebration,' he told Judy. 'I'm going to appear.'

She shook her head slowly. 'But they seemed different. Mr. Howard didn't even wave to me.'

He sighed and put his hands on her shoulders. 'I bothered them. I just couldn't see going into town and losing a day of work here on the ranch.' He grinned into her face. 'You know how I get. I just don't believe they really need me, when I have

28

more important work to do.'

'That's all,' she said, watching him. 'I wish Steve and Lottie Murfee hadn't gone to St. Louis for him to take up the law. He would have settled it without a hearing.'

Tom nodded. 'Steve would have cleaned Ned's mouth in the dust. That kid would have learned without a useless hearing that he can't spit in a man's face and curse him out.' His hands tightened on her shoulders, and he kissed her. 'Come on now. I don't want to be late. I'm driving you over to the Shields', so you can stay there until I get back.'

'Why? Do you expect trouble?'

'No. I can travel faster without you, that's all.' He nodded again to accent his words. 'Besides, you'd enjoy time with Ellen and her babies.' He glanced down at the round, firm swell of her bosom against her dress. Then he pulled her close, hugging her.

'You sure do look good to me. You'll be having enough kids of your own.' He laughed loudly, hugged her tighter. 'A woman like you is made just right to hold her man.'

CHAPTER FOUR

He did not drive the buckboard fast, for he could easily cover the fifteen miles between the Shields' ranch and Yellowstone City before noon.

Looking across the high grass as he passed his own home, he remembered his words to Judy. She did indeed look good to him, and each time he thought of the baby he felt especially fine.

He kept glancing behind him at the three-room house he'd built, thinking he would soon have to add another bedroom, and the barn would have to be made larger. He'd been lucky finding Judy in a town like Brownwood, coming to know her so well on the long trail drive north. It seemed the years of drifting, taking the good and the bad and too often having to use a gun to stay alive, had been the life of another man. He wasn't a rich man, not money-rich in terms of men like Irving Rinehart with his hotel and saloon, or Clifton Howard, or Byron Kenneally, who had brought his wealth with him from the East. He had not aimed to have that kind of wealth. He'd come here for a different kind of security. He had his own land and a wife whose every thought and act was part of him, and now the beginning of his family. That, and the security of good, close friends and neighbors were what Slattery had looked for and found.

Most of the families of Yellowstone City were at their noon meal when he crossed the river bridge and drove into Centre. He could smell chicken frying, and potatoes, and bread that had just been taken out of an oven. A group of boys played stick-ball behind one of the houses. Most of the small houses, and the business section at this end of the main street, were new, less than two years old. The livery barn, furniture store, blacksmith's, the hotel and restaurant and pharmacy, all had been added to the original buildings at Four Corners, the land office, general store, a saloon, and the two-story bank and the sheriff's office directly opposite the barber shop and harness shop.

No one moved about the walks and street. Two horses were tied alongside a buckboard at the jail hitchrail. A cloth banner, telling of the town's Jubilee Days fluttered in the breeze where it was strung above Four Corners. Beyond the intersection the Concord stagecoach had been drawn up in front of the stage office. Slattery looked around for the stage men and passengers, but he couldn't see any of them.

Then he saw the men crowded into the jail doorway.

They were the passengers who had been on the stage yesterday. One and then another of the men glanced across his shoulder as Slattery stopped his wagon and climbed down to tie his horse.

The men opened a path for him, crowding even closer together to let him come inside.

The sheriff's office was oppressively hot. Town men who had witnessed the trouble stood silently along the bare plaster walls, three of them crouched down below the gunrack. Al Wright, the sheriff, stood with the stage driver and shotgun rider in the far corner. Ned and Jim Kenneally and their uncle sat on cane-backed chairs near the barred door to the cell block. Everyone watched the circuit judge, an old man in his late seventies, question Duncan Brown from the harness shop.

'... and you ran from your shop?' the judge was saying. 'The voices you heard were so loud?'

'I heard the yells,' Brown answered. A short, thin, stooped-shouldered man, he shook his head. 'I didn't hear what was bein' said.'

'You could see the crowd?'

'I saw it was a crowd, and that there was trouble, but I didn't hear the words too clear. I crossed the street to the back of the crowd. By the time I got there, it was all over.'

The judge nodded. 'And you can't add anything to what has already been said.'

Brown's head shook from side to side. 'I wasn't tall enough. I couldn't see over the heads of the other men.'

The judge motioned him back with a flick of his hand. He shot sharp glances at the town men and stagecoach passengers. He brushed a wrinkled hand through his white hair and rubbed at the deep-lined skin of his forehead.

'It seems,' he said slowly, 'that this town is suffering with more citizens who have poor eyesight and weak hearing than any town I visit.' Not a sound was made by anyone inside the room. Somewhere in the street, a hammer pounded nails into wood, the raps of the hammer made louder by the stillness of the office. The judge picked up his gavel. 'Unless there are more witnesses...'

'There's another man.' The shotgun rider stepped away from the stage driver and pointed to Slattery. 'He saw what happened.'

Every face turned to Slattery. Ned Kenneally, his mouth swollen and discolored, an eye blackened and almost completely shut, leaned forward in his chair. His uncle, tall and handsome and immaculately dressed in a brown broadcloth suit, touched the boy's hand. Ned leaned back in his chair, and sat as quietly as his cousin Jim.

Slattery stepped to the spot vacated by Brown.

'Your name?' the judge asked.

'Thomas Slattery.'

'You swear to tell the truth in this matter? Unless you're hard of hearing and can't see well.'

'I swear,' Slattery answered. He shifted his eyes to the corner where the shotgun rider blurted, 'He was close to us. He grabbed the whip or I'd've been cut by the leather.'

Talk broke out, began to grow in

34

volume, until the judge rapped the gavel. A noisy, rough shuffle of feet and scraping of boots followed, and, at the judge's stiff glances about the room, that sound also died.

'You witnessed the fight between Mr. Ned Kenneally and Mr. William Patten?'

Byron Kenneally leaned forward in his chair, said, 'Judge Wallace, I don't believe it was a fight. If you look at the boy, and Patten, you can see who was assaulted.'

The judge stared at Kenneally. 'One more interruption, Sir, and I will hold you in contempt.'

Kenneally's sure features did not change. He nodded, and sat back. The judge again looked at Slattery.

'You witness the fight?' he repeated.

'I was on the general store porch when I heard shouting.' He told of crossing the street and going into the crowd and being close to both men when Ned spit in Patten's face, ending with, 'I grabbed Ned's arm so he wouldn't hit Patten with his whip.'

'And that is when Mr. Patten struck him?'

'Yes.'

The judge nodded. 'I believe I know

what happened after that. Thank you, Mr. Slattery.' He rapped the gavel. 'This hearing is finished. I want the court, this office, cleared except for the sheriff and the four men concerned.'

Louder talk erupted. The stage passengers and other witnesses looked at each other, and at Byron Kenneally, who stood from his chair.

'I want to stay,' Kenneally said. 'I represent my nephew and my son.'

'You didn't come in here as anyone's representative,' the judge snapped. He rapped the gavel loudly. The talk broke off and faded to a silence through which only the pounding of the hammer outside could be heard.

Judge Wallace pointed the gavel at Byron Kenneally. 'You are to leave the room the same as everyone else. You had the men who came to me in Bozeman ask for a hearing, not a trial. That's what you are getting, Mr. Kenneally.' The gavel shook at the onlookers. 'Thank you for coming in.' His gaze moved to Slattery. 'And for having me learn that except for one man, an eye-and-ear doctor could grow wealthy in this town.'

Slattery moved through the doorway

outside onto the walk. No one spoke. The stage passengers began to head toward the waiting Concord. The townsmen fanned out to go into their stores, offices, or homes. Across Centre Clifton Howard had finished nailing a large sign painted in huge black letters over the high double doors of the livery barn.

YELLOWSTONE CITY
5TH ANNIVERSARY DAYS
THURSDAY, FRIDAY, SATURDAY
AUGUST 8, 9, 10

GAMES! CONTESTS! PICNIC!
and SQUARE DANCING!

JOIN IN THE CELEBRATION!

Slattery stepped down into the roadway, then halted when a hand gripped his shoulder.

Byron Kenneally stood as tall as Slattery's six-feet-two. His straight, lean body fitted perfectly into his finely tailored broadcloth. His handsome face was as serious as it had been inside the jail.

'Thank you for appearing,' he said to Slattery. 'I wanted this straightened out, and I know you helped.'

'I told what I saw. And did.'

The fingers gripped tighter. Kenneally said, 'That is exactly what I wanted.' He smiled now and glanced across Centre. 'That should be an enjoyable time. You're bringing Mrs. Slattery?'

Slattery nodded. He felt Kenneally's hand release his shoulder, heard his, 'Fine. Fine. That's what we want, for everyone to enjoy his life in this valley.'

But the words meant nothing to Slattery.

Kenneally had his reason for stopping him and talking, to be certain his attention was on Howard's livery. Sid Rooney and a second man had stepped past the barn's open high front doors. Rooney did not wear a gun. He was dressed like any cowman, in a checkered shirt and Levi's. It was his stance and stare that caught Slattery. Rooney's eyes glared at him from under his sombrero, as though he waited, expecting something to happen.

The second man Slattery had never seen before. He was young, barely older than Ned and Jim Kenneally, big of bone with a dark face and deep sullen eyes that seemed to seek out and watch Slattery. His denim pants and faded blue shirt, wrinkled and dirty, dark blotches of sweat under the armpits, had been slept in, or he had ridden long and hard in them. The holstered sixgun thonged tight to his left thigh, the thin line of his mouth and his stare, did not go along with his working cowhand's clothes.

Slattery turned away from the pair, hearing Byron Kenneally's voice, louder now, speak to the others in the street.

'Don't go yet,' the rancher told them. 'The judge'll be through in a few minutes. You should know his decision, all of you. You've been so helpful in settling this trouble.'

CHAPTER FIVE

The men waited. Most of them remained on the walks and porches or in the street. They did not talk, simply waited, as though obeying an order.

Eddie Jones and a few of the other younger men of the town grouped around Byron Kenneally, talking to him quietly. Some of the storekeepers came out of their stores and stood on the porches, watching, waiting. Clifton Howard stayed in his barn doorway with Sid Rooney and the man with Rooney. Dick Ormsby was on his pharmacy porch, Edna and Gordon Bassett in front of their restaurant, Irving Rinehart staring out through the screen door of the hotel lobby.

Slattery crossed to the hotel. He walked up onto the top porch step. 'You told me the hearing would be held this afternoon,' he said to Rinehart. 'The judge started before noon.'

The hotel owner's round face turned left and right, to see if anyone listened. 'It must have been important enough for the judge to think he had to start early.'

'It could have been settled the way the judge is handling it now. Between the two of them.'

'Well, I told you what I know.' His stare shifted from Slattery's face to the street. Slattery looked across his shoulder.

Ned and Jim Kenneally, and then the stage driver and shotgun rider, came out of the jail. Jim Kenneally grinned widely while he and Ned, his bruised, swollen features unchanged since the hearing, walked into the crowd and began to talk.

Cheers broke out around the Kenneallys.

Eddie Jones clapped Ned on the back, joining in the talk and laughter. The stage driver had rounded up his passengers, and they moved as one group toward the Abbot-Downing Concord. The shotgun rider stood alone on the jail boardwalk. Neither Byron Kenneally nor his son or nephew as much as glanced at him while they untied their wagon and climbed onto the seat to leave town.

'Well, it's settled,' Rinehart said. 'I'm glad to see it end.'

'End?' Slattery questioned.

Byron Kenneally had swung the wagon and began to drive eastward. He paid no attention to the shotgun rider or Slattery, but both Jim and Ned threw glances toward the hotel. The hate in Ned's eyes was as cold as Sid Rooney's stare had been, as tight as the stance of the man with him. How many times had he faced the same feeling when he'd worn a gun, Slattery thought. How many times had he almost been able to hear hate as well as feel it? Like the holding tension of a rope drawn too tight.

And he'd always had to settle what had come, whether he wanted it or not.

The stagecoach passed the Kenneally

wagon. The stage driver was alone on the box. Passing the shotgun rider, the driver raised his hand and waved. Billy Patten did not return the gesture. He simply stood on the walk, alone, and watched the stagecoach roll toward the river bridge.

Slattery walked to Patten. 'You quit?' he asked.

Patten spit down into the dust. 'I was fired. We settled everything inside there. Neither of us'd prefer charges, we agreed.' He gazed toward the west at the rear of the coach crossing the bridge and going from sight beyond the trees. 'The Company doesn't want troublesome workers, and I'm finished.'

'They paid you off?'

'Three dollars. And four bits.' He shrugged his shoulders hopelessly. 'I don't have a horse, or gear, or a gun.' He glanced at the hotel. 'I don't have enough to hire a room and eat, too. Just how powerful is that Kenneally around here anyway? They wouldn't even let me sleep in the stage barn another night.'

Slattery nodded, understanding, and said, 'There are people who will help.' He turned toward the general store. 'Come with me, and we'll see what we can do.'

*   *   *

'Yes, I can use help,' Myron Blumberg said, 'especially during the celebration days.'

He pointed to the empty boxes scattered about the floor between the counters and under the shelves. He had spent the morning restocking each item on hand, marking price tags, and arranging the displays to catch the customer's eye. 'You can start by storing those boxes in my barn out back, and then give me a hand in here.'

'Thanks,' Patten said. 'I only need it long enough to buy a horse and some gear.'

'No, no thanks, please,' the small storekeeper told him. 'You'll earn it, I promise, with all the farmers and ranch wives coming in.'

Patten nodded to Slattery and began to pick up the boxes. Slattery and the storekeeper watched him carry an armful to the rear door of the long room.

'He'll give you a good day's work,' Slattery said. 'Thanks, Myron.'

'I have the cloth and other items Judy ordered yesterday.' He started up the aisle, then glanced across his shoulder at the

43

sound of the front door opening. Two small boys entered and headed for the candy counter.

'Be with you in just a minute,' Myron called to them. And, as he continued along the aisle with Slattery, 'You were over across at the hearing.'

'If that's what it can be called.' He looked at the open storeroom door. 'Patten didn't get any backing from the stage passengers. Or the town men.'

'You didn't really expect he would.'

'I expected the truth. Byron Kenneally should know he can't keep covering for those boys. I can't see why he sent for a judge. It was such a small thing.'

'Small things grow into big troubles, Tom. Byron has to have a clean slate if he plans to run in the next election. People will say he wasn't covering, but was hard on Ned and Jim, sending for a judge.'

He stopped talking, staring toward the room's rear door. A noise came through the storeroom, a low barely audible banging. Like the confused pounding of a sledge hammer, out in the barn.

'I didn't tell Patten to nail those boxes down,' Myron said. He raised his voice, called, 'Patten. Patten.'

Patten did not answer. Only the banging sounded, that and the snorts of Myron's delivery wagon horse. The mare suddenly whinnied loud, with the peculiar tone that meant pain or trouble.

Slattery and the storekeeper hurried into the back room, past extra bolts of cloth, tinned and boxed food, clothing, everything that wasn't on display. Near the open rear door a dozen well-cured hams hung from hooks. Too often the valley's ranchers and farmers lacked cash until crops came in or cattle were sold, and Myron took their products in trade. Now, Myron glanced around and saw the boys had followed them. The horse whinnied louder, beating its hoofs and rump against the stallboards.

'Stay in the storeroom,' the storekeeper told the boys. 'Don't come out here.'

Slattery saw Patten lying on the barn's dirt floor. He lay on his left side, as though he slept. But before he reached Patten, Slattery knew the man was dead.

Patten's head was twisted at an odd angle. Blood from a blow that had split his skull covered the side of his head and face.

Slattery knelt beside him and felt for some sign of life. He looked up and said to

Blumberg, 'Send the boys for Al Wright. Get him over here fast.'

He stood and walked to the horse, to calm the animal. The mare couldn't have kicked Patten, not with an iron chain hooked across her stallfront. No blood was on any of the horse's hoofs.

The barn's back door creaked and swung out at a gust of the off-river breeze, letting the hazy light of the overcast day streak in. Slattery calmed the mare and then walked to the rear door.

He didn't expect to see who had come in and beaten the life out of Billy Patten. Only bare sand spotted here and there with tufts of grass stretched to the river.

Slattery stood without moving, studying the river brush and timber, wondering if Patten would be lying dead right now if he hadn't grabbed Ned Kenneally's arm, if he hadn't acted so fast and gotten Myron to put him to work out back here where he was alone and could be so easily attacked.

Myron came into the open doorway. His thin face was ghastly white. 'He was smashed with something heavy,' he said. 'He was hit five or six times. Such a brutal way to die.'

Slattery nodded, thoughtfully, and

retraced his steps to the body.

*　　*　　*

'You didn't find what was used to kill him?'
Al Wright questioned.

Slattery and Blumberg shook their
heads. 'We looked all through the barn,'
Slattery told him, 'and out back. Not a sign
of anything.'

'Must have been an iron bar. Or a
horseshoe. Or could've been a shovel.' The
lawman gazed around at the noise of
movement near the barn's front door. The
two boys stood there watching, and talking
to three of the town men who had seen the
sheriff and the boys hurry from the jail and
come down the store alleyway. 'Myron,'
Wright added, 'will you send the kids for
Doc?'

Wright kept staring down at the dead
man. 'Had to be somethin' heavy,' he said
again.

'You've no idea who could have done it?'
Slattery asked.

'No. This is the first time there's been a
murder since I took over.'

'Dammit,' Slattery said. 'He gave Ned
Kenneally a beating. How many people you

figure would want to do the Kenneallys a favor?'

Wright stared at him. His jaw tightened, the veins in his neck stiffening. 'I don't know,' he began.

'I know. Sid Rooney was across in the livery during the hearing. Sid rode out and had a talk with me. To give me orders about how I'd better back Ned in what he said.'

'I didn't see Sid leave town,' Wright said. His jaw tightened again, his neck muscles standing out as stiff as wood, but he didn't move. Slattery was puzzled. He knew that the lawman wasn't afraid of facing a gunman. Wright's hesitation was something different. Not fear, not an absence of knowing his duty, but something more guarded.

Myron stopped alongside them. Wright kept staring at the dead man. Finally the lawman shook his head. 'We're going to the livery,' he told the storekeeper. 'You'll handle things here?'

He turned at Blumberg's, 'Yes,' and walked from the barn with Slattery.

More people had been attracted to the growing crowd, even a few of the housewives from nearby homes. Two small girls stood with their mothers. One of the older boys had raised his younger brother onto his shoulders so he could see past the grownups and tell what was happening.

'I can't see Sid doin' that,' Wright said while they passed the hotel. 'I just can't.'

'He had reason,' Slattery said. Still, he wasn't certain. His own sense of responsibility for Patten gnawed at him, made him want to stay with this until he knew . . .

'It started over such a little thing,' Wright said. 'Kids racin' a wagon like that.'

'I heard of a family feud in Tennessee,' Slattery said. 'Thirty-eight members from two families have been killed in less than twenty years. It started after the two grandfathers argued over who won a pig in a raffle. And killings over that are still going on.'

The livery's back doors were open. All except two of the sixteen stalls had horses in them. Slattery and the lawman passed the ladder to the mow before they saw Clifton Howard sat at his desk in his small office at the front of the long barn.

Howard shook his head. 'No,' he said when he was told of the killing. 'Sid

49

wouldn't beat a man to death.' He kept shaking his head. 'Not Sid.'

'He was here during the hearing,' Slattery said.

'He came in and talked to me.' Howard's eyes met Slattery's. 'He didn't cotton to you grabbin' the boy's hand. I'd say he was more after you than the stage men.'

Slattery said, 'He didn't ride out with the Kenneally buckboard. I saw them leave.'

'No.' The livery owner's bony face was thoughtful. His expression changed, concerned now. He spoke softer, choosing each word carefully. 'Sid took his horse and led it out the back way. There were four riders who came in and left their mounts.' He pointed to the nearest four horses in the double line of stalls. 'They walked out with Sid.' He nodded, his eyes and features brightening, confident and almost smiling. 'Sid was goin' to show them the back way into the hotel saloon. You go in there. He's probably havin' a drink with them. You'll see he isn't the kind to murder a man.'

*　　*　　*

The hotel saloon was long and wide and high ceilinged, with three billoard tables between the rear door and the mahogany bar that Irving Rinehart had had freighted in from St. Louis. Red and white checked tablecloths covered the ten tables which were evenly spaced between the doorway to the hotel kitchen and the bar. Pictures on the walls were of mountain lions, buffalo, deer, and other animals and birds that could be hunted in this mountain country. Behind the mahogany counter a large tintype of Rinehart and his wife and four small children, two girls and two boys, looked down from the center of the backbar mirror.

Carl Olsen, the bartender, left the four customers he had been talking to, and he walked past the double line of liquor bottles to meet Slattery and the sheriff. Sid Rooney was not in the room.

'Good to see you, Tom,' Olsen said. 'And you, Deputy. What'll you have?'

'Has Sid Rooney been in today?' Wright asked.

'No.' He pointed down the bar. 'Just those men.' He grinned. 'And Alf Porter when his missus wasn't lookin'.'

Wright and Slattery continued down the bar. The four men leaned on the counter, fingering their shot glasses or bottles of

51

beer. They had stopped their talk. Each watched the lawman.

'You men were in the livery,' Wright said to them. 'Another man was with you.'

'Man named Rooney, you mean.' The big-boned, dark-skinned man in denim pants and sweat-stained gray shirt gestured to the others. 'I was talkin' to him while my brothers were tendin' to our horses.'

'Did he come inside with you?'

'He jest showed us the door and rode off.'

'You didn't know him?' Slattery asked. The family resemblance in the four was very strong, each big-boned and dark. The oldest seemed about twenty-five or six, the two youngest clearly twins, seventeen or eighteen. Slattery went on to the one he had seen in the livery doorway. 'You were . talking with Rooney.'

The dark eyes stared directly at Slattery. 'Jest passin' talk. He said there was a hearin' goin' on.'

'What's wrong?' Carl Olsen asked. 'Nobody's hurt Sid, Tom? Deputy?'

'That shotgun rider was beaten to death in Myron's barn,' Wright said. 'Rooney left you men and rode off behind town. That right?'

The men nodded. 'Behind town, headin' out along the river,' the oldest said.

Slattery looked at Al Wright, and turned to leave. Olsen brushed one hand through his hair. 'I know Sid Rooney,' he told the four brothers. 'He wouldn't do anything like that.'

'He had reason to,' the man who'd been in the livery doorway with Rooney said. 'He thought a lot of that kid. What's his name, Kenneally?'

Olsen nodded, slowly. 'But not enough to kill a man. To beat him to death.'

The dark eyes in the dark-skinned face stared toward the door that had closed behind Wright and Slattery.

'Rooney had somethin' in for that one, too,' he said. 'He held the Kenneally kid while he was hit, and that Rooney don't seem to me like the kind who'd forget.'

*　　　*　　　*

Slattery said, 'Here, Al. I've got the spot.'

He stood from where he'd bent down to study a small grassy area among the trees. Disappointed at what he'd found, he waited for the lawman to come in from the sandy yard behind the general store barn.

53

Below the overhang of the Calligan River's banking the water swept over the sandbars and rocky shallows in a smooth even flow that for some reason sounded unusually loud.

Wright pushed through the brush. He could see as clearly as Slattery where a horse had been ground-tied. The earth had been scuffed and kicked, the grass crushed and broken by a horse's hoofs, some of it eaten. It was as clear that the rider had gone off this high side into the stream to be certain there would be no tracks to follow.

Slattery pointed to the marks dug into the sand. 'One shoe was either loose or broken.' He crouched over, drawing a circle around two, three, then a fourth hoofprint. 'See how it breaks off here, and here. The horse was favoring one of its legs.'

Wright studied the sand, and the marks, his mouth and jaw tight. 'I'm ridin' out to The Village,' he said.

'I'll go with you,' Slattery told him.

The lawman nodded. He pushed the brush aside to retrace their steps through the sandy yard and back into the general store barn.

CHAPTER SIX

Al Wright and Slattery headed east, following the course of the Calligan close enough to be able to find any hoofprints which could show exactly where a horse had left the stream and had come up onto the valley floor.

It had been Slattery's idea, just as Slattery had decided they'd make better time if he rode a horse from the livery rather than using his own buckboard.

That was part of what bothered Albert Wright.

The lawman had not missed the silent onlookers in the yard of Yellowstone City, or on the porches, or in the doorways. Each person watched him and Slattery leave. Each knew where they headed, yet none offered to join in and help.

The whole town had learned about the dead man before he and Slattery had their mounts saddled. It wasn't simply because it was the Kenneallys they meant to see. Wright believed the people just didn't have faith in him as their lawman. He had been deputy under such a strong man as Steve

Murfee, and he'd been voted the sheriff's job by the Council when Murfee resigned. But the people didn't really see him as sheriff. In fact most of them still called him 'Deputy' and showed more faith in a man like Slattery.

Now, here he was, knowing Slattery had come along because he felt a guilt about Patten's death, but he was still doing what Slattery suggested, feeling as if he trailed along for the ride more than being the one who led.

He wanted to say something about that, but didn't. Not even after Slattery angled his mount toward the trees where the river swung southward less than three miles from Kenneally's Village. They had been riding longer than two hours and a half, saying little. The horses could use a breather, and Wright followed Slattery into the brush and trees and down onto a tongue of sandbar to let the horses drink.

Slattery drew his stemwinder from the pocket of his jeans. 'Three-thirty,' he said. 'We should reach there in a half hour.'

'I'll do the talkin',' Wright said.

'I expected you would.'

Wright nodded. He rubbed his mount's neck. Suddenly the horse raised its head, shaking drops of water from its mouth.

Slattery's horse had also lifted its head, its ears stiffened. Both men, pulled their carbines from the saddle boots, knowing the horses had caught some sound.

Three riders broke from the trees above them before they could start their mounts up the banking. Ted Short, a sallow, black-browed man of about Slattery's age, led them. Will Benson and Pete Montgomery were in their mid-twenties. Each wore sixguns and had rifles or carbines in their boots. They drew up their horses and stared down into the stream.

'What's your business out here, Deputy?' Short asked.

'We're goin' to see your boss. And Sid Rooney.'

Short's cold stare shifted from the lawman to Slattery, then to the weapons both men held. Benson edged his mount closer to Short.

'Mister Kenneally'd want to see the deputy,' Benson said. 'I figure we can tell Slattery to git.'

Wright slid his carbine into its boot. As Slattery did the same, Wright said, 'Tom comes with me. All the way. Our business is with your boss.'

'After what Slattery did to Ned?' Montgomery snapped. 'Damn good thing we wasn't in town.'

Benson nodded, kneeing his mount closer to the bank edge. 'The boy wouldn't have been beaten, I tell you.' He glared down at Slattery. 'Try holdin' me like that.' He turned the thin strip of leather in his hands around the horn as though he intended to climb down.

'Slattery's with me,' Wright repeated. 'You mean to interfere with the law?'

'Well, damn me,' Benson said. 'You takin' a stand, Deputy?'

Montgomery grinned. He leaned forward and rested his hands on the pommel. 'You want some of it, too, Deputy?'

'That's enough,' Ted Short said. He motioned for Benson and Montgomery to swing their mounts. 'Mr. Kenneally'd want them to come, if they've got business with him.'

His hard stare held as he backed his horse and waited for Slattery and Wright to follow them out of the trees onto the flat.

★   ★   ★

They rode in silence, the Kenneally cowhands staying in a straight line with Slattery and the lawman.

They passed more cattle than Slattery had seen in any other section of the valley. Twenty minutes later they cut into a trail that soon merged with a road leading to the white-painted ranch houses and other buildings of the Kenneally ranch. The road showed constant use, from the deep ruts dug into the earth by the iron rims of wagon wheels. The grass on either side was lush and green, fed by two streams which flowed down from the mountains behind the area the people of Yellowstone City had come to call The Village.

Slattery could understand the nickname as he studied the buildings. Children in the yards seemed to number almost as many as in town. He'd last been out to this end of the valley longer than a year ago. One house had stood on the slight upgrade of land a mile from the eastern foothills. Now three houses, each big and sprawling, with a long, wide veranda running the length of its front, had been evenly spaced close to the timber along the course of one of the streams. A large bunkhouse was built behind the big ranch houses. Outhouses, four small shack-like homes, a blacksmith's shed, and three good-sized barns completed what seemed to be the start of a town capable of supporting itself. And more cattle grazed in the lush, wet meadows behind The Village, making the Kenneally spread easily the largest in the Montana Territory.

Ted Short kicked his horse ahead, and Benson and Montgomery dropped behind Slattery and Wright while they trotted up the long drive to the center white house. The children, nineteen of them, from babies barely able to walk to Ned and Jim Kenneally, stopped their play or work. The ranch hands, and the blacksmith, paused to watch.

Short looked across his shoulder. 'You wait in front of the house,' he said. 'I'll go inside and see if Mr. Kenneally will talk to you.'

'Sid Rooney's the one we came to see,' Wright said.

Paying no attention to the lawman, Short swung down to the ground. Ned and Jim Kenneally stepped out from among their brothers and sisters and cousins.

'What they want Sid for?' Ned snapped. His bruised face seemed even more swollen and discolored in the overcast daylight. He waved a doubled fist at Slattery. 'You should've run him off our land.'

'We're here to talk to Sid,' Slattery said.

'The deputy'll do his own talking,' Benson said. The tall cowhand turned the reins around the pommel to free both of his hands. He moved slowly, casually, as though he simply waited, but his anger was built up worse than Ned's.

'Let the deputy do his job,' Montgomery added to Slattery. 'You're jest along for the ride.'

'Get Rooney,' Wright said to Short. He leaned forward, preparing to dismount.

'You sit your saddle and wait, too,' Benson said. 'Deputy, do like you're told.'

Wright watched Short go up the steps onto the house's veranda. The smaller children began to giggle and talk. A smile came onto Jim's face. Ned's battered head nodded. Benson sat his saddle easily, enjoying Wright's hesitation.

'I'll talk to Mr. Kenneally myself,' Wright said.

Before one of the lawman's boots could clear the stirrup, Benson reached out to grab him. Slattery spurred his mount and made the horse lunge forward. It banged into Benson's sorrel mare, throwing Benson off balance. Slattery's outstretched hand shoved hard at Benson's chest, and Benson had to grip his horn and hold on to keep his saddle.

'You son—' Benson began.

'That's enough! Stop right there-'

Byron Kenneally's shouted words were an order that immediately silenced the outbreak of talk among the children and stopped Benson and Montgomery where they sat. Slattery backed his horse from the two Kenneally cowhands. The blacksmith had left his forge and crossed the wide yard. Three other cattlehands near the bunkhouse ran toward them. Through the window of the house a woman's face peered outside to watch Byron, and Sid Rooney directly behind the rancher, halt at the edge of the porch.

Benson pointed to Ned's face. 'Slattery caused that, Mr. Kenneally!' he said. 'He deserves . . .'

'He and the deputy are here to see me,' the rancher answered. 'The rest of you keep out of it.' His eyes flicked from the cowhand, to the children, then to Slattery and Wright. 'What do you want, Deputy?'

Wright stared at Rooney. 'You were in

town today, Sid. You were ridin' your stallion?'

The ranch foreman looked confused. 'You know I always ride my own horse.'

'Bring him out here.'

Rooney turned to Byron Kenneally. 'I don't know what this is all about, Mister Kenneally!'

'Jim, Ned,' the rancher said. 'Bring Sid's horse out here.' He made a wide circle with a gesture of his hands. 'You kids move back. And keep back.'

The rancher waited a few moments while he was obeyed. 'Now, Deputy. Why?'

'That shotgun rider who hit Ned was beaten to death in Blumberg's barn.' He heard the drawn breaths of the children, then the blurting outbreak of talk that was as quickly stopped by another motion of Byron Kenneally's hand. Wright went on, 'Sid was across in the livery durin' the hearin'. He rode outa town along the river.'

'I didn't,' Rooney said. 'I left by the livery's back door.' His eyes, hate-filled as Slattery had seen in town, met Slattery's stare. 'If I'd've ridden into the street, I'd've called Slattery. I cut past the Loomis house and met Mister Kenneally at the edge of town.'

'That's right,' Kenneally said. 'He was under my orders not to cause trouble.'

'We was told you went into the river brush,' Wright said to Rooney.

'I didn't. You ask Ray Loomis' woman. She saw me cut through. Her and her kids.'

'We were told.' Wright watched Slattery nod. The movement of the barn door made everyone turn and follow Ned and Jim leading the ranch foreman's horse toward the lawman. Benson and Montgomery sidled their mounts out to make room. The two Kenneallys stopped the stallion between Wright and Slattery.

Wright took hold of each of the stallion's legs, and in turn held the hoofs so both he and Slattery could inspect them. Not one of the shoes was broken. It was clear the shoes had not been changed that day. Rooney's horse wasn't the one which had been staked out behind the general store barn.

Wright looked up, his face flushed. 'Sid—'

'You can check the shoes on all of our horses,' Kenneally told him. 'Both of you.'

'No.' Wright shook his head. 'I was wrong. I figure our job's to talk with the ones who said they saw Sid go into the brush.'

Rooney didn't move, his face unchanged, his eyes glued to Slattery while Wright mounted. Benson's stare was as angry, and Montgomery's. The Kenneally ranch hands, the blacksmith, and the children, waited without saying a word. Women had come outside onto the verandas of the other two white-painted homes to watch what happened. One of the women held a baby in her arms, her face worried.

Wright touched the brim of his hat. 'We won't be botherin' you again, Mister Kenneally.' He turned his mount and started off with Slattery.

The rancher hurried down the steps and caught up with them. He kept in stride with the horses until he was beyond earshot of everyone else in the yard.

'I'll come into town,' he said. 'Rooney or the boys will go in, if you feel it's necessary.'

Wright shook his head. Slattery said, 'Why do you figure it might be necessary?'

'You've had a brutal murder,' the rancher answered. 'It's up to any citizen to offer help. I'm offering help.'

'And I appreciate it,' Al Wright said flatly. He glanced at Slattery. 'We all appreciate it.'

He kicked his horse and left the rancher, forcing Slattery to kick his own mount to catch up.

CHAPTER SEVEN

'I should've known better,' Wright said. 'To check on those men before I swallowed their story.'

'You did the only thing you could,' Slattery told him. 'Rooney was in the livery. You knew he's hot-headed and had reason to go after Patten.'

The lawman shook his head. 'Dammit, dammit, so much trouble.'

Slattery watched Wright, knowing the man didn't put all his feelings into words. It was natural they would head out to look at the shoes on the Kenneally foreman's horse. And take in Rooney if he was the one who had jumped Patten. Rooney wasn't the man, that was certain.

Slattery was as certain the valley would have rain. The overcast above the rim of the far western peaks and the flat was thicker, heavier. Late afternoon was

66

darker, the brush and timber along the river a hundred yards to their left already growing hazy with the first gray of night. They had another hour before they reached Yellowstone City. Then, he had a fifteen mile drive to get Judy to bring her home. He was glad he'd told her he might be late and to stay over with Frank and Ellen Shields if the hearing dragged out too long.

'Would have been a waste,' Wright said, again shaking his head. 'No reason to check every horse back there. If Kenneally'd been in on it, he wouldn't have been so willin' to have us look.'

'He wasn't taking chances,' Slattery said. 'Every one of his hands wore a gun. Even the blacksmith.'

'Damned good reason for that. So many kids around. And there's talk the Sioux could act up. That's why that new commandin' officer's been sent out to Fort Abe Lincoln. Man named Custer.' His gaze moved around the circle of the land, the river curving closer to the road, the brush and trees, and the dark cloud cover settled down even lower so now it obscured the highest peaks of the Madisons and Gallitans.

The first shot came in that moment. A

hard, sharp smashing of noise from ahead.

Slattery shouted, 'Down! Get down!' as the bullet ripped through his hat brim in a high whine. He fell forward across his horse's mane, grabbed his Winchester to yank it free while he dropped, hearing a second, then a third shot bang out of the timber at the river bend.

Wright crouched in the saddle, his right hand reaching for his six-gun. The second bullet slammed into his left leg. Pain slashed along his thigh, into his groin and stomach as the third slug tore a gaping hole in his horse's throat.

'Flat! Drop flat!' Slattery rolled over once, twice, clear of his horse's hoofs, seeing Wright start to fall.

Wright's body struck the earth hard. His horse moved ahead another stride and went to its knees, spurting blood and screaming in pain and terror. Slattery fired once, pumped the carbine, sent a second bullet into the spot he judged hid the bushwhacker. Return fire, a fourth, fifth, then a sixth and seventh bullets burned through the grass to find them.

Slattery rolled to the left, levered and triggered off two more shots. He lay sprawled out on his stomach, waiting, listening.

The only sounds were the pained noises from the dying horse, weak watery gurgling grunts, weaker each second.

Wright began to roll toward Slattery, but the pain made him stop and lie still.

'Bleedin' bad,' Wright said in a low voice. 'I can't help.'

'Hold tight to the leg. High on the thigh.' He could see blood seeping through the trousers onto Wright's fingers. 'I'm going after him.'

'Could be more'n one.'

'Stay put.' The horse's breathing wasn't as loud as the brush of the wind across the top of the grass. 'Use your mount for cover.'

Slattery put two more bullets into the trees and brush, then rolled fast to the left, once, twice, three times, expecting a hail of bullets.

But no shots came.

He couldn't see Wright, knew the lawman had reached the horse. The animal's grunts had stopped, leaving a complete silence that somehow seemed louder than the gunfire.

Slattery crawled forward. His hands were cold and tight. He knew the hidden enemy could not miss the movement of the grass. He covered ten yards, stopped, sprawled out as before to listen.

No sound ahead.

He fired once more, rolled over and over, the carbine pumped, his finger on the trigger.

He lay absolutely without motion. He waited for some sound, a horse neighing, nickering, one man calling to another. Nothing happened.

He moved ten yards closer to the treeline, stopped, listened, waited.

After three minutes he held out the carbine at arm's length and triggered off a shot.

Still no return fire.

Another minute passed, a second, a third. If the bushwhacker had run, Slattery knew he couldn't follow. He'd have to get back to Al Wright. His leg had been bleeding so bad.

Slattery crawled to the edge of the brush, his weapon up and ready. He pushed himself onto his knees and, crouched low, moved into the trees.

The bushwhacker had used the cover of a huge rock near the edge of the river bank. Two deep chips in the stone showed

Slattery's slugs had hit where the man's head would have been. Ten empty cartridges were scattered behind the rock.

The banking edge was scuffed where the gunman had jumped down into the black clay-like mud where he had left his horse in the stream. He had mounted in the deep water to be certain there'd be no tracks to follow.

Slattery hurried back through the trees to help Wright.

*　　*　　*

'Didn't hit the bone,' Slattery said, tightening the belt he was using as a tourniquet around the thigh.

Wright shook his head. 'You don't have to try takin' me back. Ridin' double'd be too slow.' He looked up at the sky. 'It'll be too damn dark. No chance to catch him.'

'The main thing is to get you to Doc.'

Slattery's fingers carefully pressed inches above the lawman's knee. He was sure the slug had ripped through the flesh and there would be no danger of bone fragments tearing more flesh and doing more damage during longer than an hour's ride.

He gripped Wright below each armpit

and raised him until he could stand and use his carbine as a crutch. Wright shook his head, disgusted with himself, wounded and helpless and useless.

'Easy,' Slattery warned. 'Easy now, 'til I get my horse. I'll get you back. Take it easy.'

*   *   *

Darkness was thick and damp and still when Slattery walked the horse toward the homes at Yellowstone City's east end. Wright had lost most of his strength and was bent over in the saddle, gripping the pommel to try to keep erect. The storm had struck high in the western mountains and had not blown down into the valley. Black clouds covered the peaks far below the timber line, but neither the rain nor the jagged pinkish lightning flashes and low thunder rumble would reach the town. There was little sound ahead, the low tinkle of a piano in one of the saloons, and the ringing of iron on iron as the blacksmith worked at his anvil.

It was Joe Bush, the smith's helper, who did the pounding.

Bush was a huge black man with

tremendous arms and shoulders. He paused at his work as soon as he noticed Slattery holding the lawman on his horse. He laid down his hammer and hurried along the street.

'I'll help you,' he offered, his stare on Wright's blood-soaked pantsleg. 'Carry the sheriff down to the doctor's.'

'Get Doc,' Slattery told him. 'Bring him to the jail.' Before Bush could turn, Slattery leaned down closer to him. 'Joe, go to Ray Loomis' wife. Ask her if Sid Rooney cut through her yard leaving town.'

More people saw them now, two men who stood and talked in one of the yards, a group of boys sitting at the edge of a sandy lawn betwen two of the houses, three men in the chairs on the hotel porch. The men hurried into the street to ask questions and follow the horse and riders through Four Corners. A woman pushed past the restaurant screen door. She stopped short with a shocked expression on her face, and called to others who were inside.

'We'll help you with him, Tom,' one of the men offered. 'Let him slide out of the saddle.'

'I c'n get off m'self,' Wright said. 'I'm not that bad.'

'You've lost a lot of blood, Deputy.'

'I'm not that weak, I tell you.'

Slattery stopped the horse and released the arm he had kept circled around Wright's chest. 'I'll get down, Al. Just lean off and we'll hold you.'

'Dammit,' Wright muttered looking at the upturned faces. 'I'm not bad. All this trouble.'

Slattery supported Wright's shoulders, the other men his side and legs. Wright took hold of Slattery's arm to limp onto the boardwalk. He stumbled, barely able to stay on his good leg.

'You see who shot at you?' a man asked.

Another said, 'Yuh. You know who did it, we can form a posse and hunt him down?'

'He was hidden in the trees,' Slattery told them. 'We didn't get a clear shot at him.'

He could see the doctor run up the middle of the roadway. 'Easy,' he said to Wright. 'Slow, Al. Go into the first cell. The rest of you better stay outside and don't crowd us.'

He sat Wright on the cell bunk, then checked to see how much more blood had been lost during the ride. Only a little seepage, he was sure, for the jeans had dried around the wound so the cloth had stiffened and stuck to the thigh. Wright's face was pasty white, his mouth bitten tight.

'All this trouble,' he muttered again. 'Damn fool thing.'

Doctor Hobson came into the cell. He was a tall, gangling man dressed in a conservative brown suit and spotless white shirt and collar. He set down his bag, looked at the bloody leg, and motioned to Slattery. 'You did fine getting him back.' He opened the bag and took out scissors and a bottle of carbolic acid and rolls of bandages.

Irving Rinehart pushed past the crowd at the office door. The heavy-set hotelman held a bottle of whiskey.

'He can use this, John,' he said to the doctor. 'I heard he was hurt bad.'

Hobson opened the bottle and held it out to Wright. The lawman shook his head.

'It'll help,' the doctor said. 'Take a few swigs.'

Wright put the bottle to his lips and swallowed a mouthful. While the harsh liquid burned down his throat and chest into his stomach, he swallowed a second mouthful, then leaned his back against the wall.

Slattery went into the office. 'Clear the doorway,' he told the crowd. 'Let Al get some air.'

'He hurt bad, Tom?'

The question was from Barney Akkesson, the chairman of the Council. A lean, wide-shouldered man, he almost completely blocked the doorway while he stared to see into the cell. 'How bad is he, Doc?'

'He'll be laid up a while,' Doctor Hobson answered. 'Please keep the office clear, and hold down the commotion.'

Akkesson looked at Slattery and shook his head. 'We can't go without a lawman. Not with the Jubilee Days coming up.'

'Tom, you take the badge,' Rinehart said. 'You've worn a badge before when Murfee was sheriff.'

Slattery began to shake his head.

'We need someone who'll hold down any trouble,' Akkesson said. 'Just for a few days, Tom.'

'You know what happened to the deputy.' Rinehart caught the voicing of agreement of the men who crowded the walk and doorway. 'If there's a chance of getting the one who shot Al, you'd recognize him.'

Slattery hesitated. Judy would be expecting him and would worry if he didn't come. He had work of his own to do before the baby was born. He heard Akkesson add, 'Think of your wife and the other families, with a bushwhacker loose.'

Slattery walked into the cell block. Al Wright lay with his eyes half-closed, partly from the strong smell of the carbolic acid the doctor used to cleanse his wound, partly from the result of his drinking the contents of the half-empty bottle in his hand.

'He be able to get up and around?' Slattery asked.

The doctor's head moved from side to side. 'He's lost a great deal of blood. He shouldn't try to stand on that leg for a week or ten days.'

'That's definite?'

'A week or ten days at the least. Could be longer.'

Al Wright, a slack expression on his face, watched Slattery and the doctor. He once more held the bottle to his mouth and took a long drink. Then, while Slattery waited and the doctor picked at the shreds of cloth driven into the wound by the bullet, the lawman lay quietly, so he wouldn't flinch or make a sound.

Hobson looked up at Slattery. After three years of caring for the ills and wounds of the people of Calligan valley, he seemed older than thirty-four. He nodded at the wounded leg. 'If you hadn't stopped the flow of blood with your belt, he could have bled to death. He isn't going to be doing the rounds in that street out there.'

Slattery stood over Wright. 'They've asked me to take a badge until you're better, Al.'

The lawman again raised the bottle and drank. He swallowed the mouthful, staring back bleary-eyed. "Dep'ty badge's inna desk. Mid'le draw'r.'

'It's all right with you? Akkesson will swear me in.'

"S'al'rite.' He drank and swallowed again. 'Take th' badge.'

Slattery left the cell. Wright wasn't a drinker, Slattery knew. He had finished off too much of the whiskey too fast. His jaw was as tight as it had been in Blumberg's barn after they'd found Patten. His muscles stood out as stiff as when they'd ridden away from Kenneally's Village, as though,

78

somehow, the lawman hadn't said or done all he wanted to say or do.

From the cell bunk, Al Wright watched Slattery's hazy form move to the roll-top desk, open the middle drawer, and take out the badge. Slattery stepped onto the walk through the office door. Wright downed another mouthful of the liquor he didn't even like to taste. Rinehart knew he wasn't a boozer. He'd had only one beer whenever he stopped into the hotel saloon to talk with Carl Olsen behind Rinehart's bar. The hotel owner knew that.

What the hell, Wright thought groggily. The people hadn't elected him sheriff. He'd been appointed by the Council after Steve Murfee got through, and the town would want someone like Slattery, who'd been in the War of the Rebellion and had trail-bossed a cattle drive up from Texas, and who'd taken part in gunfights.

They'd want more than they'd seen him do as Murfee's deputy, but, dammit, he could do it, he knew he could. Only now that trouble had come he couldn't walk his rounds. He wouldn't even be able to stand on a game leg.

He exhaled with a hopeless groaning noise, no longer bothering to hide the fact the doctor's rubbing and picking to clean the wound hurt like hell.

He took a long final drink from the bottle, wheezing and grunting loudly, finishing the last rotten-tasting drop of whiskey before he passed out.

★   ★   ★

Outside in the roadway, Slattery looked for and saw Joe Bush at the edge of the crowd.

Slattery's eyes questioned the blacksmith's helper. Bush's dark head nodded.

'He did,' Bush said. 'He spoke to her and the young ones on his way through.'

Slattery did not nod, nor did he answer the questions of the men who pressed in on him to learn about the shooting and Al Wright.

He pushed his way through to his horse and drew his Winchester carbine. Then, holding the weapon loosely in his right hand, he crossed toward the porch of the New Yellowstone Hotel.

CHAPTER EIGHT

Myron Blumberg hurried off his porch steps to meet Slattery in the middle of the roadway.

The storekeeper had waited until the conversation and commotion settled outside the jail before he tried to talk with Slattery. The fact that shooting had taken place outside of town was enough for many of the men to think Byron Kenneally or someone who pocketed his pay had wounded Al Wright. Blumberg didn't believe that. It was too pat, too much like a set-up, and the fact that the crowd spread out and opened a path for Tom when he drew his Winchester meant Slattery had formed his own opinion and intended to act. Myron was certain after he called Slattery's name and Slattery turned towards him and he saw the deputy's badge pinned on his shirt.

'You have a line on who shot Al?' the storekeeper asked. He eyed the Winchester, how Slattery held it, as he had seen Tom ready to use the weapon other times.

'It isn't that simple,' Slattery said. 'I am sure it was just one man.'

Blumberg's stare shifted to the hotel's second floor and the windows of the room everyone knew Byron Kenneally kept hired for when he came into town, or one or another of the women of the family stopped over to do shopping.

'Byron wouldn't bushwhack a man,' Blumberg said. 'He doesn't hold grudges.' He saw how Slattery's eyes flicked about the street, to the men on the porches, to others watching from windows or doorways, a small group of women and children among the men gathered on the residential side of Four Corners. 'I had to get after Ned and Jim last week for bothering my delivery boy, racing their wagon at him like they did the stage. Byron blasted them for that. He didn't get after me.'

Slattery nodded. 'I have to stay in town tonight,' he said. 'Judy is visiting at Frank and Ellen Shields.'

'I'll ride out, Tom.'

'Thanks, Myron. Tell her she should stay with them. I'll be out tomorrow, soon as I can.' He shifted his stance to go to the livery. 'I'm handling this only until

82

someone else can take over. Be sure she understands.'

Blumberg nodded and retraced his steps toward his store. He'd close up early and look forward to a long drive in the delivery wagon. He'd escape the steady repetition of questions he'd have to answer if he stayed open. No matter what happened in the town or valley, everyone, man, woman or child, who came into his store talked about it, more often with some far-fetched version of half-truths than the actual facts.

Slattery had crossed Centre to find him, Myron realized, and to ask for his help. Tom wasn't going to say what he thought of Kenneally, but he wanted to be certain that Judy wouldn't become worried because of his staying in town.

Myron cared about Judy's being worried, as he cared about the one who shot Al Wright being caught. He had once had a wife who was a worrier like Judy, but he had lost his wife and his baby son in childbirth. It seemed so long ago, thirty-three years, it made him feel older than sixty-two. Yet, it was still so fresh in his mind he remembered as though it was yesterday, and the hurt of the loss was always with him.

He took one final glance along the street before he opened the store's screen door. Tom was inside the livery. The black lettering of the sign Cliff Howard had nailed over his high double doors announcing Yellowstone City's Celebration was clear against the white-painted clapboards. Signs and banners, nailed up or strung from the false front of the hotel and most of the other buildings, telling of games, contests, races, and the dancing and band concert, promised something better than the grim business Slattery had to face alone.

That aloneness bothered Myron, as his being alone so long had taken its toll on him. The Council would hire someone within a day or so to wear the deputy's badge. If Judy was in town, she and Tom could enjoy everything they had planned, and as they should enjoy it, together. He wished he had realized how quickly life could change. He would have made certain he would have taken every opportunity in his own life to be together with someone . . .

He would drive out to the Shields' ranch and offer to have Judy ride back with him and use for the three days of the celebration the extra rooms he had fully furnished and so seldom used above his store . . .

★   ★   ★

'No, I don't mind,' Clifton Howard told Slattery. He lowered the right front leg of the last horse he had led out of its stall so each hoof could be checked under the light of the hanging oil lamp. 'I just believe you should have known me long enough to realize I'd tell the truth.'

Slattery did not answer. He studied the fifteen horses on the double line of stalls. None showed signs of being lathered. The bushwhacker wouldn't leave his mount in a livery barn where the owner and hostler had the solid reputation of rubbing down each animal which was brought in, and who checked each horse's mouth for cuts or irritation caused by a bit, or for saddle sores, or loose or broken shoes.

'None of the Elkins have come in since they went out with Sid Rooney,' Howard offered. 'If they had, I'd tell you.'

Slattery nodded. 'Any horses are brought in, I'll be at the jail.'

'And I'll tell you, same as I just showed you the mounts of the other two riders who came in today. Dammit, Tom. You've known me three years now.'

Slattery nodded again. 'Obliged, Cliff. I'll be stopping in.'

'You won't find Irv Rinehart any happier to be questioned,' Howard said. 'We're businessmen. We aren't going to chance losing what we've worked years to build by coverin' anyone who'd beat a man to death, or a bushwhacker.'

Slattery went out through the open front doorway, and Clifton Howard walked into the doorway and stood there watching him head for the hotel.

One man was dead, the deputy wounded, Howard well knew. But he wasn't to blame. The businessmen and ranchers and farmers who had spent months planning the Jubilee Celebration Days couldn't be blamed, nor would they go along with Slattery's badgering every visitor to the valley during these next few days.

Fliers had been sent out and nailed up all through the Territory so riders would come in for the roping, branding, bulldogging and racing events that men like Byron Kenneally, Irv Rinehart, and the Council members believed could develop into a county fair each year, something which could really put Calligan Valley and Yellowstone City on the map.

Howard shook his head, irritated at how Slattery now went into the hotel saloon porch and stopped to stare into the saloon over the batwings, then push past the screen door into the lobby. Trouble wasn't new to the people of this or any town west of Mississippi and Missouri. The only man here, besides the Kenneallys, who came from the East, was Doc Hobson. He'd seen enough that could happen from gunplay during the Goodlove trouble three years ago. Howard's irritation gradually warmed to anger. He'd seen enough trouble himself, from Indians and white men, when he'd first come into Montana Territory to try his luck working claims in the gold strikes around Bannock, Grasshopper Creek, and the Last Chance. He'd been in Adler Gulch and Virginia City and had backed the vigilante law when short work was made of men like George Ives, Boone Helm and Henry Plummer. It hadn't been like that here during the three years he'd been building his business.

He'd played everything on the up-and-up, hadn't overcharged or underworked.

He had a good mind to go to Barney Akkesson and the rest of the Council. He wasn't nor would he become part of the trouble caused by the stage shotgun rider, or what had happened after Deputy Wright was foolish enough to go out and try pushing Byron Kenneally too far.

And if he knew his men in this town, the same point of view would be taken as soon as Slattery tried to get too big behind his badge and push a man like Irving Rinehart.

CHAPTER NINE

Irving Rinehart said, 'I can't allow you to go into the rooms of my guests.' He glanced at the narrow staircase to the second floor, holding down his voice so their talk would not be heard upstairs. 'Not without asking their permission.'

'That's exactly how I want to see them,' Slattery said. 'In their rooms, when they don't know I'm coming.'

Rinehart's fat jowls tightened. The heavy-set hotelman had been seated behind the reception desk doing paper work in the flickering light of the coal-oil lamp hung above the key rack. He wore a clean white shirt, with dust cuffs over the sleeves. A thick gold watch chain swung from the pocket of his vest as he stood to step around the counter.

He said, 'I'll go ahead of you and knock on the doors.'

Slattery took hold of Rinehart's left arm. He motioned for the hotelman to stay behind him. 'There'll be no trouble, unless one of them starts it.'

Rinehart's stare dropped to the Winchester carbine. Then his stare switched to the desk. He turned the ledger for Slattery to read the handwriting.

'We had six new guests come in today,' he said, quietly. 'Nathan Elkins, Lewis Elkins, Harold Elkins, and—' He squinted to read a signature. 'Buster Elkins. The other two came in tonight. Elmer and Clay Leonard.'

'Fine. I'll talk to the Elkins now.'

Slattery moved ahead of the hotelman and started up the stairs. Rinehart made no attempt to stop him. He hurried to follow on the step below Slattery, warning, 'Those men have been in their rooms the whole evening. They ate in the saloon and went straight to their rooms.'

Once they reached the landing, Rinehart half-ran ahead of Slattery along the hallway. He stopped at the first door with the numeral 1 painted in white on the panel. He knocked.

'Yuh?' came the question from inside. 'What?'

'It's the hotel owner, Mr Elkins. Would you please open your door for a minute?'

A key clicked in the lock, and the door opened inward. The oldest of the four Elkins said, 'Sure, come in.' He stepped back so Rinehart and Slattery could enter.

Tobacco smoke filled the room. Two empty liquor bottles were on the dresser top. A half-filled whiskey bottle had been placed in the center of the card table where the Elkins twins had been playing poker with their older brother. One of the twins fingered a glass of whiskey in his hand and stared blankly at Slattery's badge and the Winchester carbine. The other took his cigarette from his mouth and waved a friendly hand. 'We been playin' stud. You wanna join us? Draw up 'nother chair, Nathan.'

The oldest Elkins' voice was sober. 'You come to talk, Slattery?' His long-boned face watched both Slattery and the hotelman.

'You been inside all night?' Slattery asked.

Rinehart said, 'I told him you've stayed in your rooms. That you haven't been out bushwhacking anyone.'

Nathan Elkins stared at Slattery as though he was shocked. He remained calm, his sun-darkened features beneath his long black hair completely controlled. His brother fingering the liquor set the tumbler down on the tabletop with a loud bang that almost broke the glass. His hair was darker than his twin, Slattery saw now, his jaw shadowed with the stubble of a beard. His twin's smile had vanished. His smooth, beardless face was wet with sweat after hours of drinking in the close heat of the room. He ground out his cigarette in the bone ashtray at the center of the table.

'What the hell are you tryin' to say?' he asked Slattery.

'The sheriff was shot outside of town. You didn't hear the commotion when he was brought in?'

The beardless face shook. His eyes watched Slattery, yet he spoke to Rinehart. 'You know we been up here the whole night. How come he can bust in?'

'That's enough, Harold,' the older

brother snapped. He nodded to Rinehart. 'He'll back us bein' in this room since we finished eatin'.' His close set eyes narrowed, but he stayed very calm. 'I'm tired of you askin' questions, Slattery. We come here to make money from some of the events you're holdin' in your jubilee.'

'You told me the Kenneally foreman left town by riding out along the river.'

'He did head out along the river.' His face stiffened when he saw Slattery didn't listen, but instead was looking at his boots and the boots of his two brothers. Slattery's eyes shifted from the boots to the gunbelts and holstered sixguns draped over the iron bedposts.

Rinehart said, 'Tom, your argument is with the Kenneallys, not these men.'

'No, dammit.' Nathan Elkins voice was harder his anger still held down while he opened the door to the room's closet. 'Look in there, Slattery. You won't find anything.' His boots thumped on the wooden floor to the door of the adjoining room. When he opened the door, Slattery could see the fourth Elkins brother and two shorter men, one bearded in his early twenties, the other older and smooth-shaven. 'You seen my brother Buster before,' Nathan continued. 'These are our cousins, Elmer and Clay Leonard. Go 'head and check them so this is finished once and for all.'

The two Leonards stood from the chairs at their card table. Buster Elkins did not move. He held an empty shot glass and wore the same sweat-stained and dusty clothes he had worn when Slattery first saw him standing outside the livery barn. His stare was just as cold and dangerous.

'Look at them, Slattery,' Nathan snapped. 'They've been in here the whole night. You've got the hotel keeper's word and our word. You ask the liveryman who's tendin' our horses. You can look in that closet, too.'

Slattery walked to Buster Elkins. He'd gain nothing by checking the closet. Mud from the boots that had made the two deep holes at the river edge would have been cleaned off. 'You told me Rooney left by the river,' he said. 'That wasn't true.'

'You callin' me a liar?' Buster leaned forward to the edge of the chair, his cold stare meeting Slattery's.

'One of you is,' Slattery said. 'Rooney will be in tomorrow to take part in the bulldogging.'

'I'm gettin' damn sick of this.' Buster stood, moving slow and flat-footed, the smell of the whiskey strong on his breath. 'We come here to make money, us and our cousins.'

'Rooney'll be in,' Slattery said again. 'I'll talk to you then.' He began to turn.

Buster grabbed Slattery's shoulder. 'You did it! You caused the trouble holdin' the Kenneally kid so he got pounded in the face! You can't blame them!'

Slattery jerked his shoulder free. 'Rooney wouldn't beat a man to death. It takes a special kind for that, and for bushwhacking.'

He heard Buster's, 'Sonovabitch!' and Nathan shout, 'No, don't!' as he turned away.

The wild-swung left fist Buster had aimed at Slattery's jaw struck his left arm, driving him backward. Buster's right came straight from the shoulder, the blow fast and vicious. He should have downed Slattery before he had a chance. But the iron barrel of Slattery's carbine hit him flush in the middle of the stomach and Buster stopped short with the fist in the air and his face going ghastly white.

Slattery backed to the wall. He held the

carbine like a club, ready to deliver the next blow.

'Help him stand,' he told Nathan.

'You bastard!' Nathan snarled. 'You set us up, you bastard!'

'Get him on his feet.' The carbine barrel made a small arc between Slattery and the others. 'Don't try anything. He attacked a law officer.'

Grunting, gasping for breath, Buster rose to his knees, then stood wobbily on his feet, one arm supported by Nathan.

'Down the stairs and across to the jail,' Slattery ordered.

'You caused that,' Rinehart said. 'Tom, I can't keep this quiet. Your fight is with Kenneally.'

Slattery shoved Buster Elkins through the open doorway toward the hall. He brought the carbine barrel around in a wider arc.

'You three,' he told the Elkins. 'I want you across in the office tomorrow to see Rooney.'

The two Leonards did not move, nor did the Elkins twins. Rinehart trailed Slattery into the hall to the landing of the staircase. One of the doors at the staircase side of the hallway had opened. A man and a woman peered out, watching Buster Elkins slow on the top stair, then be shoved so hard from behind by Slattery he had to grab the bannister to keep from falling.

'Your fight is with the Kenneallys!' Rinehart said again, almost screaming the words. 'These men here have done nothing! My other guests will swear to that!'

Nathan Elkins stepped to the hotelman's side. He looked down at Slattery, said, 'This ain't finished yet, mister. That badge ain't permanent.'

Slattery glanced up at him, and then down at Buster, his eyes taking in everything from under the brim of his flat-crowned hat.

Slattery motioned three town men, drawn from the bar by the loud voices, back clear of the hotel saloon doorway. He lowered the carbine barrel then, knowing Nathan wouldn't come after him, not now, in front of so many witnesses.

He knew, too, there was more to all the trouble than the hoorawing of the stagecoach that led to the killing of the shotgun rider and a bushwhacking. The Elkins, and Leonards riding in so close behind them, living in the very next rooms, were here for more than riding and roping.

He wasn't sure if others were part of it, Byron Kenneally, or Rooney, or Cliff Howard, or Rinehart who had made certain he shot his mouth off loud enough and often enough.

He was sure he had a vicious wolf, growling and growing meaner, by the tail, and he couldn't take a chance of letting it go.

CHAPTER TEN

Slattery led Buster Elkins along the small cell block corridor to the last cubicle. Doctor Hobson, wrapping a large bandage around Al Wright's thigh, did not glance up. Wright, still unconscious, lay sprawled on his back, snoring in a deep sleep. Joe Bush, who helped the doctor, watched Slattery pull the iron-barred door closed behind his prisoner and bang the lock shut with a loud clang.

Elkins' face hadn't regained its color, his skin grayish under the jail lamps. He held his stomach and chest and stared broodily at Wright.

'He's the lawman in this town,' Elkins said. 'He's no help to no one sleepin' it off. Who do I see 'bout gettin' out. You didn't make no charge, Slattery.'

'I said assault.' Slattery spoke the word with firm finality. The jail smelled of carbolic acid and burned lamp oil. He halted at the first cell door, added, 'He'll stay in there 'til the judge comes.'

Bush glanced at the prisoner. The doctor straightened and carefully placed the rolls of bandage he hadn't used in his black bag. Bush began to gather up the bloody bandages.

'It's best Al does rest,' the doctor told Slattery. 'He won't be going anywhere for a while. The wound is clean. The bullet missed the bone, but it's deep, and I had to probe to be sure there's no cloth or dirt left in there.'

Buster Elkins repeated, 'He's no help to no one sleepin'! I want to know who I see to get out of here!'

Slattery turned away from the cells and walked with Doctor Hobson into the office.

'Make him stay down,' the doctor said.

'I'll do his rounds,' Slattery said. 'He'll stay down.'

The doctor nodded, then stopped in the

front doorway. 'I want to examine Judy again before she's ready to deliver. I'm doing over three rooms in my house as a small hospital. You bring her in.'

'After the celebration's over, Doc.'

Hobson looked straight into Slattery's eyes. 'You be sure. I know the town mothers are talking up for a midwife. I'm a doctor, Tom. I want to be positive your baby is delivered under the best possible conditions, that it's done right.' His jaw tightened, and for the first time since Slattery had known him he realized how tired and overworked the man was.

'I'll bring her in.' He managed a grin. 'Ours will be the first baby born in your hospital.'

Hobson stepped across the boardwalk into the street. The night was dark under the overcast. The wind was chill coming off the river, blowing up dirt along the roadway, and making hazy dusty halos around the street and porch lamps. Looking across at the hotel, Slattery again wondered what Nathan Elkins meant to do, and about Irving Rinehart. The hotel owner's words sounded more like a political speech, now that he thought about it, than simple disagreement with how he backed the law.

'Mister Slattery,' Joe Bush's voice said behind him.

Bush's dark face wasn't sure of itself. The blacksmith's helper glanced across his shoulder towards the cell block. He had rolled the soiled bandages into a large ball, the dried blood bright red on the white cloth, and against the black of his fingers.

'I can stay the night,' Bush offered. 'With the sheriff down and a prisoner, I could help.'

Slattery said, 'You've been working with the smith for a year. I've been in town once a month. I've never seen you carry a gun.'

'I could bring food, and help.'

'Do you have a gun?'

'None of my own. I can learn to use the ones in the rack.' He saw Slattery was about to shake his head and added, 'That prisoner can mean trouble. I know there's six more men with him.'

Slattery swung his back to the office to keep his words from carrying to the cells. 'He has only three brothers, and two cousins?'

'He rode with six other men,' Bush answered. 'They came in across the river. I was workin' out back of the forge and saw them. Four went into the livery, and three headed east along the stream.'

Slattery put one hand briefly on Bush's shoulder. 'You can help. But not in here. Tell Mrs Loomis not to let it out she's the one who saw Rooney leave town. Don't say anything to anyone else about seeing those riders.'

Bush was disappointed. 'I could help more.'

'You'll help. You will, Joe, when the time comes. Nothing until then. That clear?'

Bush gave him a look of mixed disappointment and deep concern. He nodded and went off toward the blacksmith's, holding the ball of bandages in his right hand, as the doctor had held his bag.

Slattery stood in the doorway another minute, checking the road and its buildings. The Elkins, the Leonards, and a seventh man had ridden in together at midmorning. The same time the Kenneallys had caused the trouble with the stage. Yet Rinehart had said the Leonards hadn't come until tonight ... One man was dead, killed brutally, the town's sheriff unable to carry out his duties. It all fit together too perfectly as a basis for something to happen. But what?

He turned into the office, glad he was alone in this, that Judy was where he was sure she was safe and couldn't in any way become a part of whatever trouble he might have to face.

★   ★   ★

Trouble was on Byron Kenneally's mind.

He did not want added troubles. Too much had happened already in such a short time since Ned and Jim had foolishly caused the trouble with the stagecoach: one man dead, the man who stood for the law in the valley wounded, badly wounded from the description Eddie Jones had given after he'd ridden out from Yellowstone City with the story of the bushwhacking. And of Slattery making an arrest.

Kenneally's son Jim, Ned, and the older boys of the family, Rooney and his cattlehands, had wanted to head for town with him. But he had had only his own horse saddled and had started out alone. Now, looking ahead at the buildings of Yellowstone City, very few of them with lamps on, light shining from the windows of the jail, rooms in both the first and second floors of the hotel, and the lantern Cliff Howard always kept lit to illuminate the front of his livery, Kenneally knew he was right in not having anyone else come in with him.

The people would know in the morning that he cared enough to travel the twenty-some miles, after midnight. If he'd brought the boys, or his hired hands, it would appear he believed his family was in some way connected to the killing and shooting, or he was unsure of himself and needed to be backed. He had no intention anyone who would cast a vote on election day would believe he acted for any reason except that he cared about whatever happened in the valley, and he would always do what was best for all the people.

Even more important was to keep his family name clean. The mistake made by the boys hoorawing a stage was one thing. Beating a man to death, and bushwhacking, were completely different, crimes never to be condoned. The people had to believe, to know for certain, neither he, a member of his family, nor a man who worked for the Kenneallys, would commit such terrible acts.

Slattery had to realize that, now, and in the fall election. He had watched Slattery's face at the hearing and this afternoon in his own yard. The lawman had formed his own opinion of Ned and Jim and the rest of the family. Slattery was intelligent and tough, never to be underestimated. Kenneally slowed his horse at the edge of the town. He saw the men who waited on the hotel porch, and that they started down to the street to meet him. He thought mainly of Slattery, and what he planned to say to him.

Irving Rinehart led the five men with him to a spot in the middle of the road. Kenneally could do nothing except stop and talk to them.

Rinehart's face was haggard, needed a shave. In spite of his tiredness, he looked confident. His voice was strong and loud.

'Byron, you've heard about the killing and the deputy,' he said. 'I knew you'd come in. Your room's ready at the hotel.'

'I'm going to see Slattery,' Kenneally answered.

Rinehart's fat face moved from side to side. 'I don't know what Tom is trying to do.' He motioned to the men behind him. 'Slattery has one of their family locked up and won't let him out.'

Kenneally nodded. 'Eddie Jones rode out to our ranch and told me. The judge...'

'My kid brother ain't goin' before any judge,' the tallest of the men said. He did not wear a gun, but Kenneally saw how his right hand dropped to his hip, a habitual motion Kenneally had seen only too often since he had brought his family west. The four men with him stood as loosely, their hands at their sides, in perfect response to their leader.

Kenneally said, 'I'll talk to Tom.'

Slattery was in the sheriff's office doorway, a carbine in his hands, waiting for him.

'You have a prisoner,' Kenneally said after he dismounted and stepped onto the walk.

Slattery nodded, his eyes on the men in the street. 'You brought in the judge for Ned. You can send for him again.'

'You're not holdin' my brother!' Nathan Elkins shouted. The words rang through the night silence like a gunshot, echoing into the alleyways.

'Go back to the hotel,' Slattery told the men. The rifle barrel glinted in the lamplight. 'Mr Rinehart, you can come in. Not them. I want them off the street when I make a round of the town.'

'I'll stay here.' Rinehart's words were as loud as Elkins'. 'You can't make special laws for special people. We'll stay here.'

Kenneally followed Slattery to the office desk. The rancher looked at Wright asleep in the first cell. Buster Elkins watched from the last cell, his face pressed against the iron bars.

'Nobody from my ranch shot Al,' Kenneally told Slattery. 'None of my family or my ranch hands left after you rode off.'

'I figured you'd say that to the judge.'

'It's the truth. It's exactly what we will say.'

'That everything you rode in for, Mr Kenneally?'

Byron Kenneally looked straight at Slattery, seeing much more than the tall, dark-tanned and grim-faced man who met his stare as tightly. Slattery wasn't just hard and tough, he was also monumentally stubborn, and there was only one way to reach him. It wasn't by complaining of the burden of raising your own family and the family of your dead brother, being a

106

protector to the women and children, and the families of those who worked for you.

Kenneally said, 'I brought in the judge so the boys would realize they have to face responsibility for every act they do.'

'Even spitting in a man's face?'

'Even that.'

'And racing a wagon?'

'Yes, dammit, yes!' Kenneally snapped, the deep frustration and anger in him blazing out. 'That's why I'm sending everyone of them back East to college when they're old enough! Male and female, Slattery. I believe we all have a great deal to offer in our lives, and education is the basis of that.' He nodded to accent his words. 'I'm running to represent this Territory in Washington for just that reason. I believe a railroad line through the valley will give it the growth it needs. I believe I did the right thing about Ned.' His head shook as confidently. 'Nobody from my ranch bushwhacked you and Wright. Now, you have the facts.'

He swung on his bootheels. Buster Elkins' shouts followed him to the doorway. 'What 'bout me? I didn't do nothin'!'

Kenneally stared across his shoulder. Al

Wright continued to snore behind Slattery, and beyond him Buster Elkins' nose and jaw jutted desperately through the bars.

'I had the judge for my own,' Kenneally said. 'The law is the same for you.'

He heard the prisoner scream an obscene curse at him, knew the words carried to the town citizens who were awake. Such a minor act causing all the trouble, a buckboard racing at a stagecoach, even causing him to lose his temper. He wanted a large majority vote in the fall. Time enough to plan for that after the trouble settled. Kenneally cleared his mind of all emotion, thrusting anger and doubt to the back of his mind, calm again.

Rinehart waited in the street, his tired, unshaven features worried. He stepped forward, close to Kenneally, and glanced across at the five men on his hotel porch.

'I've kept them quiet,' he said. 'I'm afraid, Byron. They could cause real trouble.'

Kenneally said, 'We've a lawman to handle them, or anything that happens.'

'I heard them talk. They're mean. They heard you tell their brother he won't be let out.'

'The judge will be here the first of the

week, after the celebration.'

'That's just it,' Rinehart said in a thin, high voice. 'I think you ought to cancel the jubilee.'

'We can't cancel. You know the railroad people are going to visit during the weekend to see what we do have to offer in this valley.'

'I don't care,' Rinehart said, emotionally.

He glanced around at Slattery closing the jail door before he began a round of the town. He looked toward the lamplight which had suddenly gone on in the room Ben Harper used as a home above his saddlery, then finally at the men on his hotel porch. 'You're on the Council from your end of the valley, Kenneally! You should meet with the Council! Postpone it, anyway!'

Kenneally shook his head. He looked directly at Slattery, and spoke in a controlled, quiet voice.

'There will be changes made,' he said. 'I'll see to that. But the jubilee goes on in this town as planned. Exactly as we planned.'

CHAPTER ELEVEN

Rinehart walked alongside Byron Kenneally toward his hotel, both men aware that Ben Harper hadn't closed his window but continued to watch them. The Elkins brothers, the Leonards, and two other hotel guests, a man and his wife who had been attracted by the loudness of the voices, stared from the porch and out the window of their room and followed the silent strides of the rancher and hotelman.

Once they reached the porch, Rinehart grabbed Kenneally's arm and stopped him. 'You have no argument with Mr. Kenneally,' he said to the five men. 'He represents the Council.'

'I don't care 'bout any Town Council,' Nathan Elkins snapped, his voice raised to be heard the length of the street. 'My kin ain't appearin' in any court.'

'He'll do what the law requires,' Rinehart told him before Kenneally could answer. He kept hold of Kenneally's arm while they moved up the steps and passed the men. 'I may not agree with Mr Kenneally, but I'll back him and the

Council along with every other man in this town.'

Kenneally paused after he pulled open the lobby door. He turned to Nathan Elkins and said, 'I don't think your brother will be given more than a fine.'

'How 'bout bail?' Nathan questioned. 'He come here for the bronc-bustin'. He c'n still take part in that?'

'I'll talk to the Council.' Kenneally looked at Rinehart, and the hotelman nodded.

'He should be allowed bail,' Rinehart agreed, and he continued to nod while Kenneally went inside. 'I told you your argument wasn't with that man.'

The younger two Elkins clearly weren't satisfied, nor were the Leonards. Their eyes followed Nathan's grudging stare towards the west end of Centre where Slattery walked through the livery's lighted work area to check the barn doors. Nathan spit down at the roadway before he swung around and motioned for the others to go into the lobby ahead of him.

Rinehart continued to stand at the edge of the porch. He shook his head, listening to the metallic grating of the screen door hinges when the door swished shut. He listened for and heard the window over the saddlery being closed by Ben Harper.

Then, Rinehart glanced toward the darkness beyond the livery. He could not see a movement in the night made even blacker by the overcast, yet he knew Tom Slattery was there, checking locked doors, making certain the town was safe, and letting the people know they were safe.

The thought ran through Rinehart's mind that a man, one man, could carry out whatever he intended successfully, if his plans were well thought out, well made. He had had the thought often before. He believed in it, depended on its certainty as he strained his eyes to catch some sign of movement to be sure Slattery continued his round the way he knew Wright would have done.

He caught sight of Slattery now, the man's tall body a hazy blur of shadow crossing the width of Centre.

What one man can do, Rinehart thought once more. One man ... He nodded to himself, the inner feeling of certainty stronger in his mind than it had ever been, while he turned away from the west end and pushed open the lobby door.

Slattery kept his stride slow. He did not

fool himself. He might have been too quick to take on the badge and carry out Al Wright's duties until the Council hired someone else as temporary deputy. But he did wear the badge and the responsibility was his, right down to the completion of the round of the town now, and the round he'd have to make after daybreak.

The seventh rider who'd come into Yellowstone City bothered him. The Elkins and Leonards he could see, one in the cell and the rest at the hotel, he could handle. His problem was the seventh man, learning why he had stayed out on the flat somewhere. He could be the one who had bludgeoned the shotgun rider and who'd shot Wright.

Walking up the restaurant steps to check the door, Slattery watched the hotel. Rinehart had left the porch lamp lit, so the street was partially illuminated, as was the livery work area. Except for the wide yellowish squares of light streaming down from the jail windows, that side of the roadway was dark. Even the second story of Ben Harper's saddlery was pitch black and blended into the heavy overcast. The very silence of the deserted walks and road seemed to hold a threat, as though the

113

intense quiet could conceal a trap.

He'd been bushwhacked once, knew the one who'd laid and waited for him and Wright had had a patience that could be used out here. He held the carbine pumped, his finger on the trigger while his eyes probed the mouths of the alleyways between the buildings, the porch roofs, the intersections of the streets.

People were still up, he knew, especially the town husbands and fathers who had been awakened by the loud voices. He'd seen three window shades edged aside while he passed the east end houses. Only the slightest glint of a light streak had showed, long enough for a peek outside before the shade was dropped back into place. People were worried, their fear as real as the mingled smell of the dry dust and the river dampness.

Slattery slowed as he moved off the restaurant steps. He thought he had caught a movement near the blacksmith's, a slight shuffling of something, or someone, in the dark.

Thoughts of Judy and the baby swept through his mind, that he shouldn't be out in this street, alone. Fear trickled coldly down his spine. He bent forward, going into a crouch, the carbine barrel centered on the blacksmith's closed door.

Joe Bush's thin body was pressed against the wood of the building so he couldn't be seen from the street.

Slattery slowed to make it appear he simply tested the locked door. 'I might have shot you, Joe. I thought you'd gone home.'

Bush's eyes flicked up and down the roadway. 'Someone was inside, Mr. Slattery. While I helped the doctor. I had just finished makin' two shoes, and one's gone.'

'You're sure?'

'I left them beside the forge when you rode in with the sheriff. One was taken.'

'Thanks, Joe. Go home now. Let me get a good distance away from you.'

Slattery continued ahead, the chill along his spine changed to an icy cold. He kept to the outer edge of the walk and moved at an even slower pace. It all had to do with what went on in the town, the killing and bushwhacking part of it, but leading to something that had to come. Six men had ridden in, each of them on edge, gradually moving in, pushing, pushing so he'd had to lock one of them inside a cell, while the others kept up their talk and pushing.

Then the full impact of the threat struck him.

The seventh man hadn't had time to fix his horse's shoe after he'd killed Billy Patten. Slattery was sure he and Al Wright had been trailed to Kenneally's. There had been ample time for tending a horse's broken shoe while the commotion had been centered in front of the jail. Wright couldn't move. Only he and Myron Blumberg knew the horse staked out by Patten's killer had a broken shoe. And Myron had driven out to see Judy . . .

He was in mid-street. One window showed a lamp still burned behind a drawn shade on the hotel's top floor. It was Byron Kenneally's room.

Slattery altered his stride toward the hotel. Suddenly he crouched, listening. The sound he'd heard in the silence made him drop forward, throwing himself flat, his hat falling from his head while he aimed the carbine at the thick darkness of the alleyway alongside the restaurant porch.

The gunshot from the alleyway came like an explosion, the barrel flash level with the ground. The bullet struck the top edge of Slattery's left shoulder, tearing like the

116

slash of a red-hot blade.

Slattery let out a cry of pain. He triggered off a shot and caught the high-pitched sharp hurt yell of his attacker. He rolled to the right to escape the next bullet, but the shot didn't come.

Boots kicked, a man groaned and grunted in the alleyway's darkness. Slattery rolled to the right again, intending to lever another cartridge into the chamber. Knotting, sickening pain tore down his arm. The shocked fingers of his left hand loosened on the weapon, then tightened while he lay without movement to catch his breath.

Running boots thumped, away from him in the alley. The retreating attacker stumbled and fell against the restaurant clapboards. He regained his stride, was running hard and heavy as Slattery pushed himself to his knees, then onto his feet to follow into the blackness of the alleyway.

CHAPTER TWELVE

Irving Rinehart pushed past the screen door of his hotel lobby and moved out onto the porch. He halted at the top step and studied the street. Centre was dark except for the two areas where lamps threw yellowish patches of illumination. In front of the restaurant the flat-crowned hat the hotelman knew was Slattery's lay twisted over on its brim. Nothing else was in sight or moved. He could hear no sound along the entire length of the roadway.

A half-minute had passed since the last shot. The only noise was behind Rinehart, loud voices of men and a woman and heavy thumps of feet on the staircase, exactly as he'd known it would be inside his hotel after the first gunshot blasted the quiet of night.

Boots thumped across the thick wood of the lobby floor. Rinehart moved down to the bottom step before Byron Kenneally rushed out onto the porch.

'Someone shot at Slattery,' Rinehart told Kenneally. He was calm, in complete control of himself. He was always in control, he prided himself on that. He did now, stepping into the street with Kenneally. 'I was working in my office when the shooting started.'

Kenneally ran toward the hat. It lay like a dead animal, Rinehart thought, awkward,

118

the brim twisted under the flat crown.

A full minute had gone by now, without another gunshot.

While Kenneally reached down to pick up the hat, Rinehart saw windows brighten up and down Centre, the townspeople over their shock, wanting to learn what had happened. Rinehart heard the lobby screen door swish open with its loud metal rasping, then the voices of the Elkins brothers, the Leonards, and the middle-aged Winston woman who had taken a room with her husband yesterday, all asking questions, confused, the woman's words high-pitched, nervous and frightened.

Kenneally straightened. He held the flat-crowned hat in one hand and pointed a finger of the other hand at the dirt in the street.

'Slattery was wounded,' Kenneally said.

The small damp spot that darkened the dirt was blood, Rinehart could see. He nodded his head. He looked around at those on the porch.

'Don't come down here,' he told them. 'Tom Slattery was shot.' None of the Elkins or Leonards had guns. The Winstons, both wearing bathrobes, edged backwards toward the safety of the lobby. Rinehart added, 'Go inside, all of you. Please stay inside.'

Kenneally took one stride toward the dark mouth of the restaurant alleyway. Then, he halted. He brushed his right hand down his side, the motion used by so many men who wore weapons.

A second minute had passed, and no more gunfire had sounded.

'I don't have a gun,' Kenneally said. 'We should help the sheriff.'

'Yes.' Rinehart turned. 'I'll get us guns.'

'You want me—' Winston began. He quieted when his wife gripped his arm. 'No, Gordon, you're not a lawman! We're here to start their school! Not for this!'

Rinehart hurried up the steps with Kenneally. He swung one arm out to include the entire street, Ben Harper coming out of his saddlery front door, and three other town men who headed toward them from the residential section. 'We'll help the sheriff,' the hotel owner told the woman. 'We'll take care of our own.'

Gordon Winston nodded. His wife's small face turned to watch Kenneally hurry into the lobby. Her lips trembled. She held her husband's arm tighter.

'This trouble started because of you!' she called after Kenneally. 'Those boys of yours started it! You have a great deal to answer for, Mr Kenneally!'

Rinehart kept moving behind Kenneally. He knew the rancher had heard the shouted words. Those who ran along the street had heard, Harper, Barney Akkesson, Cliff Howard, Banker Lashway, Joe Bush, at least three more men he couldn't see clearly to identify but who ran up from Four Corners and were close enough to hear. And to remember and talk about it tomorrow.

A third full minute had dragged out, Rinehart judged. No shots came, no way to know if Slattery lay dead or bleeding to death or was walking into the sights of the bushwhacker hidden somewhere out in the dark.

'I have two sixguns in my office!' he called to Kenneally. 'Hurry, so we can get out there and help Tom!'

*   *   *

'Tom! Where are you, Tom!'

Rinehart's shouts swept loudly along the street and echoed down through the alleyway where Slattery crouched waiting, listening for some movement some sound from the one who'd shot him.

Another man in Centre answered as high-pitched and excited, 'He's out behind town! Tom's chased him up the alley!'

Boots and shoes kicked and thumped, the men crowding together to rush into the darkness between the buildings.

Slattery crouched lower, waited in the hope the noise and confusion would force the bushwhacker to leave his cover and make his break.

Three, four minutes he'd stayed in this one spot, not daring to try to cross the open yard between the alley and the barn behind the restaurant. He had no idea of the exact spot the gunman had chosen to duck down and wait for him to show himself, nor did he have any illusions about himself. The badge he wore wasn't the only reason he'd become a target. He'd made his own enemies in the past two days, and his being killed would settle a lot of problems. Thoughts of Judy rushed through his mind, mental images of her and the baby that made him curse his taking the badge he'd had no right to take, not with a wife, and a baby coming . . .

He edged backwards deeper into the darkness. The noise of the men killed all chance of his hearing the bushwhacker, giving the gunman time to get away. Slattery straightened a moment before the man in the lead could reach him. Pain tore like a white-hot needle down across his left shoulder and arm and weakened the fingers that gripped the Winchester.

'Stop!' Slattery called. 'Don't go into the open!'

He held the carbine level across the width of the alley so the leader would bump into the weapon and stop. It was Byron Kenneally. The tall rancher slowed as he struck the Winchester but then was forced another step forward by the others bunching up and pressing him and Rinehart, directly behind him, against Slattery.

'You see him?' Kenneally questioned. 'We're here to help.'

'He's out there in the dark,' Slattery said. 'Don't try to go after him.' He raised his voice to be heard at the rear of the crowd. 'Don't bunch up. He puts a shot in here, he'll kill one of us.'

Confused talk, scuffing of feet, the men's bodies brushing against the buildings,

123

made him shove the carbine hard into Kenneally's chest. 'Take this. Hold them back.' He raised his left hand to his shoulder and gripped his wound. Warm slippery blood trickled onto his fingers, down along his palm. He drew his Colt, said to Rinehart, 'Fire high at the barn to cover me while I cross the yard.'

In that instant someone carrying a lighted lantern ran from the street into the alleyway, and just as foolishly dangerous, another lighted lantern appeared, waved above the holder's head. A savage thrust of fear drove through Slattery. He and every man near him was silhouetted plainly against the blackness of the night.

'Douse the lamp! Put it out!' A man at the rear swung his fist and sent one of the lamps sailing through the air to smash in flames on the street.

No shots came from the barn beyond the alley.

'Keep back, all of you,' Slattery ordered.

'I'll go with you,' Rinehart began.

'No. Stay with the others. Keep quiet, all of you!' He moved to the end of the alley, his spine pressed flush against the restaurant clapboards, his left hand gripped tight to his shoulder.

He was almost certain he'd draw no gunfire as he edged around the corner. Still not absolutely sure, he crouched down to offer less of a target.

No shots came. No sound, no movement. He heard only the rustle of his own clothing and his own heavy breathing.

Keeping low, he started across the yard. He'd hit his man, he saw now. Dark spots of blood left a trail in the dust, leading toward the far corner of the barn.

The bushwhacker was hit badly. He'd tripped and fallen near the barn door. Streaks of blood and scuffed earth showed he'd crawled to the side of the barn and laid there and waited with his weapon aimed.

Slattery straightened. He exhaled, partly to relieve the pain in his shoulder, mainly because of the realization he wouldn't have had a chance if he hadn't stopped in the alleyway. He pictured Judy, alone with the baby, the two of them alone because of his own carelessness and damn-foolishness . . .

'He's got away,' Rinehart's voice said behind Slattery. 'No sign of him, Tom?'

The other town men had followed the hotelman and Byron Kenneally into the open. They were half-dressed, wearing trousers or jeans, some barefooted with their nightshirts tucked under their belts or hung down to their knees. They stood stiff-legged and stared around as though they did not know what to do next.

'He was wounded!' Rinehart said. 'Good work, Tom! He won't be back!'

'We could spread out and make a search,' Kenneally offered. Three of the men picked up the idea and began to move out fanwise. Slattery stopped them.

'Irving's right,' he said. 'He's hurt and will keep running. Go back to your homes and families.'

'But he'll get away,' Kenneally argued.

'I don't want one man going after him in the dark,' Slattery said. He stared intently at the men's faces, then into the darkness beyond the buildings, his own face deadly serious. 'Go ahead. Go home to your families.'

Holding his shoulder, pressing at the pain and seepage of blood, he waited while the men turned. And he followed them into and down through the blackness of the alley.

CHAPTER THIRTEEN

Walking alongside Slattery, Irving Rinehart was silent, calm, yet he was filled with a sense of satisfaction and accomplishment which grew with each step he took.

He had watched Slattery's face, had been close enough despite the dark, that he could see something he'd never believed he would see.

Slattery was afraid!

The one man, in addition to Byron Kenneally, who had to be stopped from acting, was Slattery. Rinehart had known it since the first moment he'd made his decision to become the power in Calligan Valley, in this entire area of Montana Territory. He had almost done that. It was almost complete. He'd heard the first words of the people against Kenneally, who believed he had the election sewed up. And Slattery, the man who'd led a migration of whole families from Texas along with their entire herds of cattle, who had faced down the most ruthless gunmen ever to come into the valley, the man the people believed in and took orders from without question, had lost his nerve.

Rinehart saw that even clearer now, leaving the alley, just as he saw the clouds had begun to break toward the north. Slattery did not speak to anyone, simply continued his slow stride into Centre to cross and go into the jail. The acting lawman didn't want to go into the dark again and chance being killed. He knew it, the other men knew it, even Kenneally, still carrying Slattery's Winchester carbine, realized the wounded man had made his decision to look out only for himself.

The strength Kenneally had had would be gone when Slattery left town and rode to his home. The talk started by the Winston woman would spread, just as word would spread that it was Irving Rinehart who wanted to postpone the Jubilee Days. The people would remember the trouble was started by two of the Kenneallys, running down the stagecoach. They would remember the shotgun rider had died because he stood up in court and testified against the Kenneallys, and Al Wright had been wounded on the return ride from the Kenneallys' Village. Byron Kenneally had made the long ride himself, alone, during the middle of the night. Kenneally would have his story to explain his reasons, yet talk would spread he had to be in town to be certain Slattery was taken care of.

Doubt. That was what won or lost elections. Rinehart was positive the doubt would win for him. Each man who headed back to his home now would have questions, he was sure. His sureness was in the slight nod he allowed Nathan Elkins while he walked up the steps onto his hotel porch. Elkins, his brothers, and the Leonards, had carried out their part of the plans to this moment. They would do what had been planned for tomorrow.

'You got a trouble town,' Nathan said before Rinehart reached him.

'Too troublesome for the likes of us,' his darker-skinned, whiskered brother agreed. 'We git Buster out of your jail, we're not stayin' 'round for your jubilee.'

'If I have my way,' the hotelman answered, 'there won't be any contests for you to enter. I've disagreed with some of the Council on this since the start.'

He turned away from the Elkins and the Leonards, and nodded to the Winstons who watched and listened through the screen door from the safety of the lobby.

Rinehart was even more confident, aware of the strained expression on the woman's face, how she stared at Byron Kenneally out in the roadway beyond the porch steps.

Kenneally had paused to glance across at Slattery in front of the jail. Doctor Hobson had not let Slattery unlock the door to the sheriff's office. The doctor looked at the wounded shoulder, and he motioned for Slattery to accompany him along the walk toward the darkened east end of town to his office.

Rinehart turned again, to go into the hotel lobby. He had seen Kenneally start after Slattery and the doctor to return the Winchester. He had seen the rancher's face. Kenneally was so worried and confused about all that had happened, his actions and excuses would only add to everyone's doubts.

What Rinehart did not see, as he let the lobby door swing in and slam loudly behind him, was Clifton Howard running through the darkness at Four Corners to catch up with and stop Slattery and hurriedly talk to him.

★　　　★　　　★

'You found blood?' Slattery said to Clifton Howard.

'Outside the barn's back door, and on the latch.' The livery owner breathed in deeply to regain the breath he'd lost running. 'I was going to go inside after the shooting to make my final check for the night. I heard the horses first. They don't usually make a commotion. Someone has to be in there.'

Slattery watched Howard thoughtfully. He pressed the ache in his shoulder, glanced back along Centre. Byron Kenneally was the only person in the street. Every other man had returned to his home. The Elkins and Leonards had gone into the hotel with Rinehart. Kenneally walked directly toward the intersection, the Winchester carbine gripped tight in both of his hands.

'Tom, you should have your wound bandaged,' Doctor Hobson said.

Howard said, 'If it is the one who shot you, he's been hit bad.' He stared across his shoulder as Kenneally reached Slattery. 'You have to get him out of my barn.'

Kenneally heard the last few words, and understood. 'I was going to offer to cover the town while you were at the doctor's,' he told Slattery. 'I'd like to go with you now.'

'Tom, you've lost blood,' the doctor said.

'Come with us, Doc.' Slattery nodded to Kenneally. 'Stay behind me with Howard and the doctor.'

'It wasn't my man who shot you,' Kenneally said.

'Stay behind me, all of you.'

Slattery went diagonally across the intersection, keeping himself and the three men in the dark. Blood on the livery doorlatch was enough for him to know the bushwhacker was badly wounded. He cut down the Loomis' lawn, then moved through the adjacent yard, his strides slow and careful, so they'd not give the families in the houses reason to look outside. If there had to be gunfire, he didn't want more people caught in it.

The valley floor beyond the outhouses and barns they passed was dark and silent. He wasn't able to see anything except the few feet of sand ahead. He could hear only the touch and brush of the off-river wind against the wood of the buildings. Far to the west, beyond the screening timber of the Calligan, Judy would be asleep and both she and the child within her were safe and apart from the trouble. He was thankful for that.

He and Judy had taken the first three days of their marriage as a short trip out along the southern pass into the valley. They'd stayed in the stone cabin Ernie Gibson had built high up in the foothills for his workers who felled and stripped the trees he cut at his sawmill. He and his new wife had lain in the absolute quiet after their first time of love, warm near the fireplace and smelling the sweet scent of the pine while they talked.

She had wanted her own children ever since she could remember as a girl growing up in the Central Texas plains. And her own home. She'd talked of that. He had listened, content and happy that he had only the life of a rancher ahead of him, knowing the depth and feeling of her even more than he had ever believed he could know in another. He wanted what she wanted, and they'd loved and talked and planned until they both hadn't realized night had passed and together they'd watched the darkness fade and morning light work down from the mountain peaks into the thick growth of timber, all warm and golden and wonderfully silent, like a promise of the good that was to come . . .

★   ★   ★

Snorting of horses carried through the livery's rear door. Lamplight showed as a thin yellowish streak at the door's bottom. Slattery moved even slower, his right hand holding his drawn Colt raised to keep the others silent. Kicks of hoofs and louder noises of the horses' rumps bumping the stall boards gave a clear warning someone was still inside the barn.

Slattery pressed his back against the four-by-four of the door frame. He barely touched the latch with his thumb and felt the slippery cold wet of blood. He gripped his shoulder tight, deadened the pain, then flipped the latch up and flung open the door.

A man, his body almost doubled over, had one of the horses out of its stall. He had put a saddle on the stallion, but was having trouble with the cinch. The horse lifted its neck at the sudden noise of the door banging inward. The man swung around and cursed. His hand let go of the wide strip of leather and began to drop to his holstered sixgun.

Slattery was on him, the Colt barrel swung down onto the man's head. The man fell, and Slattery could see why he'd been bent over while he tightened the cinch.

His entire left side from his chest to belt line was drenched with blood. His wound had slowed him with the horse, yet it didn't slow his mouth from lashing out a steady stream of obscenity at Slattery.

'Who are you?' Slattery snapped, the Colt barrel raised to slam again. 'Why are you here?'

'He's badly wounded,' the doctor warned. 'Tom—'

Slattery's raised arm held the doctor away.

'Who are you? Why me?'

'Tom.' Doctor Hobson started to kneel on the barn's dirt floor alongside the man. 'I'll take care of him.'

The man cursed again. His long whiskered face was twisted in pain, the eyes wide and hate-filled. He rolled to the left as though he meant to move closer to the doctor, but instead his right hand reached for his sixgun.

Slattery's right leg shot out. The booted foot caught the man at the side of his head. The man's fingers let go, and the weapon

135

dropped and went sliding through the dirt. The man sprawled flat on his back, groaning and gasping for air. Slattery towered over him.

'Who put you on me?' Slattery kept his legs spread, stood flat-footed, not allowing the doctor to touch the wound. Kenneally and Howard stayed clear of Slattery. They watched him carefully. Slattery realized his voice was hoarse, his words more of a snarl than a question. 'Who?'

'Go to hell.'

'You'll go! Right now! Who!'

The man cursed, shifted his weight to try to sit. Slattery's foot came off the ground. He leaned forward to drive it into the pain-twisted face.

'Tom!' Hobson screamed. 'No, Tom. You'll kill him!'

Slattery hesitated with the foot in mid-air. He felt Kenneally's hand grip his shoulder to hold him.

Slattery lowered his foot and edged backward. He looked at the doctor, then at Kenneally and Cliff Howard. He exhaled a long, slow breath from deep within his body. He stared again down at the doctor. Kneeling, Hobson was bent over the chest wound blocking out the man's head and face.

Slattery stared at his own hands. His fingers trembled, a slight shakiness that was part of the chilling sensation which had made him need to draw the long, deep breath.

He'd never felt this way before, not in the war, not when facing down gunmen who were on their two feet holding a weapon or ready to draw on him. Judy was on his mind, their child, the man lying before him, the town and valley, all confused, yet somehow deathly clear . . .

'Get a blanket,' he told Kenneally and Howard. 'Carry him to the jail soon as the doc has him ready.'

'He should be in my hospital,' Doctor Hobson said. 'He's too weak.'

'To the jail,' Slattery repeated, the hoarseness in his tone sharp and definite. 'He lives, he stays right where I can watch him.'

CHAPTER FOURTEEN

Centre Street was dark and still. The gunfire that had ended almost an hour ago was already forgotten as far as Nathan Elkins could tell. To the north over the mountains the clouds had broken so the barest trace of stars showed through. The light they gave was veiled, hazy, and it was the only light Slattery would have besides the few street and porch lamps and the yellowish flattened squares thrown from the jail windows down into the sand. There'd be no moon. One of the reasons Nathan had gone along with the plan Rinehart had laid out was the certainty there'd be the full cover of the dark during the next two nights.

Standing in the window of the hotel room with the shade up, Nathan didn't use caution. He did not care if he was seen. Slattery was wounded. Cletus had done his job. He'd gotten away, and Nathan just waited for morning to come. The slow, step-by-step buildup Rinehart had planned had made Nathan, his brothers, and his cousins bored and restless. They were ready to act.

Somewhere out in the street voices sounded. Nathan pressed his forehead and nose to the glass and watched Four Corners.

Slattery would go back to the jail. He'd

be a perfect target, would be seen clearly under the lantern that illuminated the street intersection. If the man had to be finished off, now was the time, Nathan thought. He would take his Spencer rifle from the closet behind him. He couldn't miss.

But Rinehart didn't want it done now. Nathan didn't like the fat hotelman, yet he had to admit Rinehart had the knack of making certain nothing could go wrong. He had judged exactly when the stage was coming into the valley, that the Kenneally boys wouldn't miss a chance at raising hell by hoorawing the driver. A killing in the general store would be tied to the Kenneallys, after everyone in town knew the old storekeeper had blasted the boys a few days before for doing the same thing to his delivery wagon.

There were no holes in the plan. The deputy had been put out of the way, not only wounded, but dead drunk and useless in his self pity. Buster had been locked up, giving the family reason to come down on the law and the town, and the people would blame Kenneally.

Nathan's nose was sore, pressed hard against the glass. His face was wooden, his eyes tight. The voices were louder. They didn't come from Four Corners, but from the other end of Centre.

The dark figures of men moved into his view. Led by Slattery, two of them carried someone in a blanket, with the doctor following alongside.

'Oh, no!' Nathan said aloud.

He looked around. He'd blurted the words before he'd thought. Lewis and Harold slept soundly. Through the open doorway between the rooms he could hear Clay and Elmer snoring and wheezing. They couldn't possibly wake up and see outside.

Nathan went to the door, opened it, and closed it behind him without a sound. He moved down the staircase as silently.

If it was Cletus on the blanket, if he was hit, he had to know. Buster, Lewis and Harold he could hold down, and Elmer, too, he figured. Clay was the man he couldn't control.

He didn't knock on the door of the small office behind the lobby desk. Rinehart wasn't asleep on the canvas cot he used when his family was out of town. The hotelman bent over some papers and a ledger under the desk lamp. He glanced

140

around and stared at Nathan.

'You shouldn't come in here like this,' he began. 'If anyone saw you.'

'Get out here. Look at this.'

Nathan's words, low and sharp, made the hotelman follow him from the room, through the lobby, to the front window.

The four men, Kenneally and Howard straining under the weight in the blanket they carried, had reached the jail doorway.

Slattery unlocked the door, then stood aside to allow the others to pass and enter the office ahead of him. He held his Winchester carbine in both hands. If his shoulder wound would slow him from using the weapon, he didn't show it.

'That could be my cousin.' Nathan's words were a low whisper.

'No, he got away.'

'Someone's been hurt. We didn't go along for somethin' happenin' to one of us. You better find out.'

Rinehart scowled, rubbed his jaw, not liking the hard tone of Elkins' voice, as he hadn't liked the man walking in on him. 'I can't. They can't think I'm watching.'

'Think? Who the hell cares about what they think? Is my cousin hurt? We want to know.'

Rinehart pulled back from the suddenness of the man's explosive fury. 'The doctor's with them. He'll take care of anything.'

'I have to know!' Nathan reached out and grabbed the front of the hotelman's white shirt. 'Clayton's still asleep upstairs! Before I have to tell him, I want to be sure! You know why, mister!'

Rinehart didn't move. Noise, louder voices, any confusion would bring the other guests down. 'I'll go across. At daybreak. As though I have no idea what happened. There's no danger, with the doctor there.'

'Soon's the sun's up!' Nathan said. He pulled Rinehart's veined face closer, his eyes shining in the light from the porch lamp. 'You find out, or all hell's goin' to break loose a lot sooner than you want!'

★　　　★　　　★

'Into the middle cell,' Slattery told Kenneally and Howard.

'I'd have more to work with in my home,' the doctor began.

'He goes in the cell.'

Slattery could see the man in the blanket was unconscious. The office lamplight

142

glinted on the wide blotch of red blood that had already soaked through the bandage the doctor had wrapped tight around his middle. The man's bony, whiskered face seemed to have little color, the cheeks sunken and hollow, the lips slack and still.

Al Wright groaned on his cell bunk. He opened his eyes, his stare confused until he was able to become fully aware of the reason for the movement and talk which had awakened him. He pushed onto one elbow, looked from the man being laid on the middle cell bunk to Slattery.

'What happened?' He exhaled in a long, slow breath. 'Oooh, m'head.'

Slattery saw the lawmen's pained grimace. He also saw the expression on Buster Elkins' face. The prisoner in the last cubicle had sat quickly, his hands rubbing sleep from his eyes. Now, Elkins stood and stared down through the iron bars at the wounded man. His eyes were glued to the man's face, his own expression surprised and concerned.

'You know him,' Slattery said. He laid the Winchester flat on the office desk and walked past the middle cell. He stopped close to Buster Elkins. 'Who is he?'

Elkins shook his head.

'Tom,' the doctor said, glancing around at Slattery. 'I'm going to have to take care of him first. How's your shoulder?'

'I can wait.' Slattery watched Elkins, aware of the throb in his shoulder yet not bothered by it. Elkins dark sullen face couldn't be read.

'Who is he?' Slattery repeated.

'I don't know who he is,' Elkins answered. 'Just leave me 'lone. Dammit, leave me alone.'

Slattery watched the prisoner back from the bars and lie down on the bunk and close his eyes. But Slattery thought of Buster's first reaction. He had calmed and he also thought of the livery barn and the wounded man and the horse he'd had almost saddled.

They'd been watched coming in from the livery along Centre. He'd seen a movement in one of the hotel's upstairs windows. Someone had watched.

They'd have visitors, Slattery knew. He knew who had made the trouble, and how many of them there were. The only question was which one of them would come first. Then, after that, exactly what they would try to do . . .

CHAPTER FIFTEEN

Rinehart was the first to come. The sun hadn't yet risen above the eastern peaks, but as soon as the barest hint of light showed beyond the mountains and clear daybreak was not many minutes away, the hotel front door opened and Rinehart stepped outside and started across Centre.

Slattery walked, to the office door.

Behind him the doctor sat beside the bunk of the unconscious man. Buster Elkins was the only one in the office who had slept, or pretended sleep. Kenneally and Howard had stayed inside the jail the entire long night and early morning. Very little had been said, even by Al Wright, sober now but weak from his wound and unable to do more than lie quietly and watch with the others. And to think.

Slattery had had hours of thought. He had not kept control of himself in the livery, or he would have realized then what was happening in the town. He would have known it was one of the Leonards' horses the wounded man had saddled, and that the only horses which caused a commotion in their stalls were the ones not belonging to either the Leonards or the Elkins. The horse the bushwhacker had chosen knew him. It had not shied away or kicked or offered trouble to the man who had intended to use it for his escape.

Rinehart stepped onto the walk in front of the office. Slattery opened the door.

The hotelman moved past Slattery. 'I thought you and Al would be hungry, Tom,' he began. 'I thought I'd have food brought over.' He stopped, looking at the doctor and the wounded man, then at Kenneally and Howard. 'What is this, Tom?'

'He's the one who bushwhacked me.'

Rinehart's round face studied the cell block. 'You hit him, that's right. Will you need more help?'

'Just food. You go across and get it ready. For four of us.' He nodded to Kenneally and Howard. 'They're leaving right after you.'

'We'll stay,' Kenneally said. 'If you think he wasn't working alone.'

'I'll get more men,' Rinehart offered. 'Akkesson, Gibson, Lashway. Gus Vierra and Lute Canby will come in from their ranches.'

'We'll handle it,' Slattery told him. 'We would appreciate the food. You go back across.'

'Of course. Of course.' Rinehart moved to the doorway. 'I'll come over again.' He glanced down at Buster Elkins. 'His brothers and cousins might want to talk with him.'

'Of course, Irving. Whoever wants to see him.'

Rinehart nodded briskly. Howard and Kenneally started to follow him. Slattery touched Howard's arm. 'In a half hour, Cliff,' he said, 'go out along the river. I think you'll find a horse staked out in the brush. Put it in your barn behind your own horse, and let me know.'

'I will.' He moved off across the walk, but Kenneally hung a few steps behind him.

'It wasn't one of my men,' the rancher told Slattery. 'Not in Myron's barn, after you left my ranch, or last night.'

Slattery met the tall man's direct stare. 'I don't figure it was,' he said.

He stood in the doorway, as though he paused to breathe in the morning air. The sun was coming up, and everything had bright light upon it. And he could see the shadow of movement behind the same hotel second story window where last night a man had stood and watched the street.

Rinehart saw Nathan Elkins watching from the window.

He would remain calm. He had to stay calm, yet he couldn't understand how everything had suddenly gone wrong. After all his plans. Except for the stage shotgun rider being killed instead of Myron Blumberg, there hadn't been a hitch. That had been better for him, actually. The people had even more reason to tie the beating to one of Kenneally's men. But Slattery, damn him! He'd known he'd have to get rid of Slattery, as well as Kenneally, but, damn him, even without knowing, Slattery had done the one thing that could mean an end to his plans!

No, not an end. A change, not an end.

Pushing open the lobby door, Rinehart once more had that thought flash through his mind. Not an end. Just a change. The men upstairs were too deep in, with Slattery smart enough to realize who had killed the shotgun rider and wounded both Wright and himself. Time was on his side. The family had reason to go after Slattery. It could work out even better for him.

The people would remember it was Irving Rinehart who argued against, and that it was Byron Kenneally who had backed, the idea of opening the roping, riding and bulldogging events to outsiders. Kenneally was to blame for any trouble caused by those outsiders. The people would remember when he announced his candidacy against Kenneally to represent the Territory.

Nathan Elkins waited at the door of his room. The instant Rinehart entered he saw Clay Leonard stood in the middle of the room. The Elkins twins and Elmer Leonard waited near the bed, their faces as tight and serious as Nathan's and Clay's. 'My kid brother over there?' Clay Leonard asked. He was bare to the waist. A jagged, purplish scar ran the length of his ribs on his right side. But it was his tone of voice and the steel-hard stare, not the ugly-looking scar, that made the hotelman stop short.

'He's been wounded,' Rinehart answered. He looked at Nathan. 'Slattery knows you're going across to see your brother.'

'How bad is he hurt?' Clay asked.

Rinehart said, 'The doctor stopped the

149

bleeding.'

'How bad is Cletus hurt?'

Rinehart stood alone in the close silence of the room. He knew he was absolutely alone, that his plans could die right here. He could die right here. He could sense it from Clay's tone, from the way he stood. He'd met with Nathan in Bozeman, had made his deal with Nathan, but it wasn't Nathan but Clayton Leonard who controlled the family from the start. That was why his brother Cletus had been chosen to do the shooting, why the Elkins had ridden in first to look over the town, making certain everything was clear for Clay and Elmer.

'He's been shot and has lost some blood,' Rinehart said. He thought the man would curse, or swing out and hit him. But Clay Leonard only nodded.

'Can he ride?' Clay asked.

'I didn't see the wound. He was lying down. The doctor's with him.'

'He was bandaged?'

'Yes, he was. Yes, he's not that bad. I don't think he is.'

Clay turned to his brother, then to Nathan. 'We'll get him out,' he said. His tone remained calm, his eyes calculating, judging time, the town, the jail across the street. 'The money we were to be paid,' he went on to Rinehart. 'I figure Cletus and Buster have done enough to earn it.'

'The bank doesn't open—'

Clay Leonard hit Rinehart, his left fist slamming into the fat man's stomach. His right struck more viciously, dug in deeper before Rinehart's knees started to buckle. Clay grabbed him by both shoulders and kept him on his feet.

'You'll get the money. We'll have to lay low while Cletus is mendin'. We'll need money.' He looked at Lewis Elkins. 'Saddle our horses and have them ready out front.'

Rinehart wheezed and grunted to regain his breath. He stood in the middle of the room, not moving, not daring to move, watching Clay put on his shirt and then both he and Nathan buckle their holstered sixguns around their waists.

Clay took Nathan's Spencer rifle from the closet. 'Slattery's alone in that jail with the doctor,' he said. 'Nathan, you and Harold'll come with me.' He handed the Spencer to his brother. 'We'll need time gettin' Cletus on a horse, Elmer. Cover the street out there. Slattery or anyone else tries to stop us, cut him down.'

★   ★   ★

Inside the jail Al Wright swung his legs off the cell bunk and lowered his feet to the floor. He hadn't spoken in the past half hour, nor had Buster Elkins or Doctor Hobson.

The bullet had torn through the top of Slattery's shoulder missing the bone by a fraction of an inch, leaving a bloody, painful gash. During the ten minutes since the doctor had finished cleaning the wound and putting on a tight bandage. Slattery had sat at the office desk. He had opened the top drawer, then the other drawers, and he'd gone through the contents until he found the back-dated wanted posters. Some were torn and yellow with age. He had separated five from the rest, two which had sketched pictures of them, three that gave the descriptions of gunmen and other criminals in large black letters.

'I can use both legs,' Al Wright said into the drawn-out silence. He eased himself onto his right foot and balanced his body so he wouldn't fall. 'See, Doc. I'll be fine.'

'You're only using the good leg,' Hobson

warned. 'Put too much weight on the thigh, and you could bleed again.'

'No, I won't. Look.' He took a step which was more of a hop on the right leg. When he tried to support himself on the left foot, he grimaced and reached out to grip the cell bars with both hands.

'Lie down,' the doctor told him. 'You're not strong enough yet.'

'No. I can do it. I can.'

'Al, lie down.' The doctor glanced at the unconscious man on the bunk. He could barely tell he still breathed. He had changed the bandage when blood seeped through. The new bandage was tighter and so far no red showed. But it was too soon to be sure. 'I have enough to do caring for him, Al. Lie down and don't make things worse.'

'Dammit,' Wright said. 'I should be up. Tom has to make a round. I'm good enough to sit at the window.'

Slattery turned in the chair and looked at him. Wright had shaken off the effects of the liquor, yet pain from the pressure of his weight on the wound dug deep lines at the corners of his mouth.

'Rest, Al,' Slattery said. 'Doc's right. You need time.'

He caught the lawman's muttered, 'Dammit! Dammitall!' while he again bent over the lower drawer and arranged the wanted sheets with the five he had separated on top.

He continued to bend forward, feeling the dull throb in his shoulder, tired and uncertain. He hadn't found a dodger for the wounded man. Nor were there sketches he could tie definitely to the Elkins or the Leonards. The sheet he kept on the very top, its edges thumb-bent and the paper brownish-yellowish with age, could be the older of the two Leonards. And for his guess, the man in the cell bunk was a member of that family.

He couldn't figure out why they had come to Yellowstone City. Hired guns didn't compete in ranching events which paid twenty-five dollars top money. Too much had happened, the attack on the stage driver, the sheriff being shot, a try at killing him, all following each other so closely it seemed to be part of a plan. But why? He rubbed his forehead and thought of how a stampede starts, first one steer or cow getting spooked or excited and beginning to run, then another and another until a whole herd followed and broke and stomped and crushed everything and anyone in its path. With beatings and shootings already taking place, he feared even more what could happen once the street outside the office was filled with the people of the town and the families of every rancher and farmer who would drive in for the celebration.

'Tom,' Doctor Hobson said, 'There are some men who're going to come in here.'

Slattery stood, his shoulder forgotten. Each of the three men who crossed Centre from the hotel, Nathan Elkins, one of his twin brothers; and the older of the two Leonards, wore guns.

Slattery picked up his Winchester and stepped around the desk. He stood with the back of his legs braced against the desk-front and held the carbine leveled, waiting for the door to open.

Clay Leonard entered the office first. His left hand stayed on the door knob, his right hand at his side. His face showed innocent surprise at the sight of the carbine's muzzle aimed directly at him.

'Watch it!' Buster Elkins called from his cell. 'He shot that poor kid! He'll shoot you!'

'Take off your guns,' Slattery ordered.

And when Clay's right hand reached down toward the butt of his Colt, 'No, unhitch the belts. Drop them.'

Nathan Elkins stopped on Clay's right, his young brother to Clay's left.

Slattery's carbine muzzle centered on Clay's throat. 'Drop them, I said.'

Clay's eyes didn't leave Slattery's face. He would have given the exact same orders as Slattery. His respect for the man had started the instant he'd stepped into the office. Slattery was edgy, would carry out the threat, knowing even a slight neck wound would finish him. The deputy sat up in his bunk, a sixgun in his hand. Clay knew his two cousins sided him, but facing two guns, at least two of them would go down, possibly all three. It wasn't worth the gamble. He kept his hands clear of his Colt and began to unbuckle his gunbelt. His cousins unbuckled to drop their guns.

Buster was saying in a shrill voice, 'He shot that poor kid! Rotten bastardly thing to do!'

'Talk to him,' Slattery told Nathan. 'He keeps a civil tongue. You better convince him.'

Nathan walked past Slattery. Clay took a step to follow. Slattery jabbed with the carbine muzzle and stopped him. 'It's his brother, not yours.'

'He's my cousin,' Clay said flatly. 'He's in my family, I back him.'

'You'll back from right there. You and Harold.'

Slattery watched Clay. Clay's stare was hooded and controlled, yet the man was as edgy as he was himself, Slattery knew. Clay's eyes shifted to Nathan and Buster. He was interested in the wounded man, an interest Slattery felt more than Clay's expression showed. Now Clay's glances took in the entire jail, the white-washed stone walls, the cell block, the rear door, even the iron, pot-bellied stove and the wood pile behind it.

'When's the judge comin' back?' Clay asked Slattery.

'Monday.'

Clay nodded, his eyes on Buster and Nathan at the end of the cell block. 'You'll be comin' out,' he told Buster. 'Don't you worry.'

'Five days is too long,' Buster said.

'The law's the law,' Clay answered. 'You'll just get a fine. Stay quiet, these lawmen, even the doctor'll have to say you didn't cause any trouble.'

157

'That's what I told him,' Nathan said. 'We got no argument with the law.'

Buster nodded. He had suddenly grown mild, and backed from the bars to sit on the bunk.

Clay waited while Nathan left the cell block. His eyes again took in the entire jail, resting an instant on the single barred window high up in the rear wall. He looked at Slattery. His voice and face were expressionless. 'Obliged,' he said. 'A man's family's in trouble, he wants to help.' He turned and bent to pick up his gunbelt.

'Leave them here,' Slattery told him. 'We have a no-gun law in this town. They'll be returned when you ride out.'

Nathan and Harold Elkins stood with their gunbelts at their feet. Both watched Clay. Clay straightened. His mouth was set. He was particularly calm.

'You'll take care in here,' he said. 'You wouldn't want to lose your prisoners.'

'That's why the doctor is staying. We don't intend to lose anybody.' Slattery did not move from the desk, the carbine still held level.

Clay studied the cell block, his stare on the doctor. 'That's good. Good. A doctor shouldn't ever lose anybody.'

158

He led Nathan and Harold through the doorway and across the walk. The town was just coming alive. Columns of smoke rose into the almost cloudless sky to show the wives and mothers were getting breakfast. A lone man, probably a store-keeper, turned into Centre from the residential section. Clay visualized the town in an hour or two, with the people out to begin their celebration, wagons from the ranches and farms full of the families who would come to shop and enjoy the first day's events.

'Lewis has the horses.' Nathan said alongside Clay.

Clay had seen their horses waiting in the hotel alleyway, just as he saw Elmer waiting behind the curtain of the building's upstairs room. He was glad Slattery was smart and careful. It would have been too much of a chance if Elmer only winged him and Slattery was able to close the jail door. The five of them couldn't break or shoot their way into that solid stone fortress.

A cold, deep shiver ran down Clay's spine. Not the iciness of fear, but something else. Cletus was hit bad. He would die unless he was taken where there were doctors with more than two or three

159

years' experience, where they had the know-how to save him. And if that young Hobson did bring him through, there'd be a hangman's scaffold waiting for him at the intersection of Four Corners, not the bandstand that was to be erected after the races ended.

'The law's got to make a round,' Clay said. 'Lew'll hold the horses out back 'til Slattery steps outside.'

'We got our rifles,' Harold began. 'He won't stand . . .'

'A wagon,' Clay said, cutting him off. 'We'll need a wagon to move Cletus. The one they use for deliveries from the general store is the best I've seen. It has a heavy canvas top.'

'The storekeeper rode out of town last night,' Nathan said.

'He'll be back.' Clay glanced up and down the wide street. More men appeared from their homes. The first man had reached his hardware store and was busy lowering the gray awning to shade the walk.

'The business they expect today,' Clay went on, 'he'll be back with his wagon. We got no worry there.'

CHAPTER SIXTEEN

'I can stand,' Al Wright said for the fifth time. 'My leg doesn't hurt like it did.'

'You can't walk,' Slattery answered. 'You wouldn't be any good to me in the street.'

'But I can help.'

'Doing what?'

'Covering you. You shouldn't be alone out there.'

'There's no other choice.'

'There is. I could stand on the walk. I could watch your back.'

'And you'd be a wide-open target. Like a duck in a shooting gallery. That isn't smart.'

'It isn't smart for you to go alone. It just isn't.'

'Al's right,' Doctor Hobson told Slattery. He had kept out of the conversation, his attention on the unconscious man, and watching how Buster Elkins listened to the two lawmen argue. The prisoner enjoyed their disagreement, confident a split between the two would be to his advantage. The doctor looked steadily at Slattery, whose face was almost too controlled, brooding and angry, the anger part of each word he snapped at Wright. 'If you won't use Al, other town men will be willing to help.'

'And if there is trouble,' Slattery said. 'Who's going to explain to the women and kids how their husbands or fathers or brothers got killed?' He held the Winchester carefully in both hands, stared through the front window into Centre, mulling over his own reasoning and deciding it was as solid as when Wright had managed to support his weight on his bad leg and limp into the cell block corridor. 'I'll make the round. Lock up after I'm outside.'

'Dammit,' Wright said. 'You can't last the whole day. You haven't slept.'

'I'll last. Until the Council meets to replace me.'

'You think they'll want to keep me, too,' Wright said, 'if I stay in here nice and safe?' His voice carried no conviction. 'Some sheriff, I am.'

'You got no worry,' Buster Elkins put in. 'All's my family wants is for me to be let out. Let them come in.'

'Feet first!' Slattery snapped. 'That's the

only way any of them will get into this jail.' He swung the Winchester toward the cells, causing a sharp stab of pain in his shoulder, his stare on Buster, then the man on the bunk. 'He's one of yours, mister! They want both of you! They won't get you!'

Buster backstepped fast from the bars, fear lining his face. He didn't try to answer this man who had the same reactions he feared in both his brother Nathan and Clay Leonard.

Slattery turned again to the window. He realized suddenly that Al and the doctor were right. He was very tired, and violence wasn't what he wanted, not the kind of violent thoughts going through his mind right now. It wore him out and made him sick to his stomach.

He stared broodily through the glass. More people moved along the street and walks. Cliff Howard headed across Centre from the work area of his livery. Howard seemed as normal as Ben Harper, who opened the front door of his saddlery and then reached up and straightened the cloth Jubilee Days Celebration banner strung from the building's false front.

Howard's face wasn't calm when Slattery opened the door. 'I found the horse,' he said. 'It's got a broken shoe.'

'I told you to put it into your own barn at home.'

'I did. Tom, all the Leonards' and Elkins' horses are gone from the stables. My buckboard's gone, too.'

Slattery nodded. 'Go to the restaurant and have them spread the word to stay off the street. Everyone off the street.'

'Tom, I said the buckboard's gone—'

'Spread the word,' Slattery repeated emphatically. 'Keep the hell out of the way.'

He did not shut the door after Howard retraced his steps into Centre.

He had to go out, and make the men who surely watched from the hotel realize nothing would be different in the town. He'd seen the horses in the hotel alley, knew why they'd been saddled and now probably waited in Rinehart's barn. The buckboard, too, stolen so the younger man could be moved. They intended to take him . . .

If he should die here . . . He'd had the same feeling near the end of the war. Word had been spread Grant and Lee were meeting to talk of peace in a courthouse at Appomattox. After coming through so many skirmishes and battles there had been so much to live for, and the fear of dying he'd felt at the very end then was no different from his fear of dying now and leaving a wife and baby, so much to live for . . .

He looked back into the cells. Without another word he stepped outside and pulled the door closed. Damn the Jubilee Days, bringing in this trouble! Damn them! He gripped the Winchester in both hands, his anger held down, smouldering. He cursed whatever it was inside him that drove him to do what he had to, his own fear a part of it, forcing him to go on . . .

'He's headed east,' Clay Leonard said. He edged back from the hotel room's window and turned to Nathan and the others behind him. The Spencer rifle he'd taken from the closet felt good in his hands. The two Colt revolvers Rinehart had brought from his office, one in Nathan's hand, the other held just as ready by Harold, more than made up for the weapons they had left inside the jail.

'Wait'll Slattery goes past after he checks Four Corners,' Clay went on. 'Harold, Elmer, cut wide out around the intersection and get across behind the jail. Once we

165

start shooting, as soon as we get Slattery, come up on each side to smash in the door.'

Elmer and Harold went into the hall. Clay nodded to Rinehart.

'Come here.'

The hotelman moved quickly. He had done exactly as ordered. His plans to be elected to office no longer existed. Only the need to live controlled his mind, and Clay controlled his body and actions.

'Look down there,' Clay told him. Rinehart stared through the window. The street never looked so wide and empty, never was such a threat to him. Then, Clay's words struck him like a blow to the stomach. 'You'll go down onto your porch. Call Slattery over to talk to you.' He smiled into the hotelman's bloodshot, puffy eyes. 'Nathan will be with me in the lobby.' He gestured with the Spencer at Nathan's Colt. 'Get Slattery to stop out beyond the bottom step.'

'You'll warn me?'

'I'm warning you now.' Nathan continued to smile. He jabbed the muzzle into the fat stomach. 'You be ready to drop. Now, you know what to do.'

Rinehart led them into the hallway. He walked to the door nearest the top of the staircase and knocked. He did not wait for the door to open. He walked to the third door from the room he had just left, and knocked.

The Winstons, husband and wife, were fully dressed when they opened their door. Both man and woman stared wide-eyed at the sixgun Nathan leveled at them.

Byron Kenneally opened his door and stood in the doorway holding a Starr revolver in his hand.

'I figured you'd be up to something,' he began.

'You didn't figure we'd let you stay up here behind us.' Clay motioned to the gun. 'Give that to me.' His Spencer rifle was centered on Kenneally's throat. He had the same smile that had split his lips when he'd spoken to Rinehart. He nodded at Nathan's revolver, and the Winstons. 'Try anything, and they die, too.'

The woman's gasp and her husband's terrified stare were enough for Kenneally. He lowered the sixgun.

Clay took the weapon and jammed it under the belt of his trousers. 'Follow Rinehart. All of you.'

Rinehart moved toward the staircase landing. He dragged his feet, paused there.

He looked at Clay as though pleading for a last-second change of mind. Clay's hard eyes flicked toward the lobby. Rinehart clenched his fingers into fists, opened them again and, holding onto the bannister, started down the stairs.

*   *   *

Sunlight streaming down through the broken clouds in a golden, pastel softness warmed the wide green stretches of valley grass and timber, taking the dampness from along the river so a mist steamed out of the banks, a thin, transparent whiteness that lazily shifted and drifted in the small off-water breeze.

But the goodness and beauty of the day were lost to Slattery while he made his turn at the far side of Four Corners. Having Cliff Howard spread the word to keep the street and walks clear hadn't worked. More and more people, too many of them women and children, were out. More would come, with the wagons which would bring in the ranch and farm families already on the trails and roads. He couldn't stop them.

A man entered Centre from Cross Street. Russ Mifflin, who clerked in Herman

Webster's hardware store, walked slowly. He raised one hand in a wave and quickened his step to meet Slattery.

Slattery said as soon as he reached him, 'Weren't you told to stay inside today.'

Mifflin squinted against the sun. 'You got the man who shot you, Tom. I have a job to do.'

'You be ready to close up. Tell Herman.'

'We have guns inside. You want help?'

Slattery shook his head. 'Just stay inside and keep everyone inside if there is trouble.'

He let Mifflin move ahead of him. He could spot men at each end of town and at the ends of the side streets to turn people back. Yet some would still come in, and the men would be in the open to make easy targets. Too many clear targets.

He slowed his stride, giving Mifflin time to reach the hardware store before he approached the hotel. Clay Leonard and Nathan Elkins would hit from the corner of that building, he was certain. The store clerk was inside, and Slattery quickened his pace, staying to the middle of the road, his hands tight on the Winchester, his finger curled around the trigger. His eyes switched back and forth, up and down, to watch everything at once, first and second story windows, the false fronts, the lobby doors.

He was past, safe and sound, but his body shook and a cold sweat ran across his shoulders, down his spine, under his arms. They were tricky, the Leonards and Elkins, trying to throw him off. They had guns, their horses saddled, a buckboard with the horses hitched. They had to act when they had him in the open. Maybe that was it. He'd walked in mid-street, showing he expected they'd come out shooting.

He moved in closer to the buildings on the left. He passed the barbershop, the livery, the blacksmith's, and approached the homes at the town's west end without turning to look back. If they wanted to play it slow, he wouldn't give them a sign he grew jumpier and jumpier each minute.

The sun was hot across his back, then the heat and bright shine a burning glare when he swung around to retrace his steps up the roadway.

He walked past the houses and approached the blacksmith's and the livery, his eyes squinted against the sun. A mile out to the east beyond Four Corners the first wagon headed in. The driver on the seat was still too far away from him to tell who drove it. A man and a woman went onto the porch of Blumberg's General Store. They tried the door, found it was locked, then looked in through the windows to learn why Myron hadn't answered their knocks or opened up. The blacksmith's barn doors were closed, but smoke rose from the chimney showing Joe Bush was inside. Slattery still could not see a movement in or near the hotel.

He angled more to the left and the jail walk.

Then, his heart slowed, he slowed his stride, bringing up the Winchester.

Irving Rinehart had pushed past the hotel front door and stepped onto the porch. Slattery had expected one of the Elkins or Leonards to rush out, shooting. His heart continued its beat, thumping in his throat.

'Tom,' the hotelman called. 'Can I talk to you, Tom?' His raised hand waved and beckoned for Slattery to come closer. 'I need you over here.'

Slattery turned toward the hotel, watchful, the carbine still aimed.

The yells and first shots didn't start in the hotel. Slattery hardly understood what happened, the gunfire erupted so fast from the jail. It came with a crash of glass breaking, and the bang of a carbine, its echo resounding from the building fronts into the alleys as a second, then a third shot blasted.

'Run! Slattery! Move! Quick!' Al Wright's voice yelled, screaming as he continued firing, sending bullets across into the hotel.

Rinehart had dropped and was sprawled flat on the porch. His body hugged the wood. Bullets from guns inside the lobby zinged past Slattery, one slug pulling at his pantsleg while it tore through. Slattery zig-zagged, put a shot into the window alongside the hotel door, levered another cartridge into the chamber and sent the bullet through the door.

He caught sight of a man charging up the jail alleyway at him. He swung the Winchester as he ran, almost to the jailwalk now, and he shot Harold Elkins in the leg.

Harold stumbled, tripped, and fell forward near the alley mouth, his revolver still gripped in his fingers.

Slattery charged at him and kicked the weapon from his hand. He held the Winchester in his left hand and grabbed

Harold's arm with his right. Pain slashed across his shoulder while he yanked and pulled and half-dragged Harold onto the walk.

Wright's cover fire had been joined by another gun inside the jail. The two weapons banged out a fusillade that had driven the gunmen in the hotel behind cover.

The jail door swung in. Slattery, bent low, held Harold in front of him as a shield. He was almost to the open doorway when Elmer Leonard appeared from the other jail alleyway. Elmer's Colt was raised, aimed, but he did not fire.

Slattery's arm circled Harold's neck to keep him on his feet. Harold screamed, 'Don't shoot! Don't, Elmer, you'll hit me!'

Slattery's carbine motioned into the jail. 'Get inside!' he told Elmer. 'You'll die right here!'

Elmer dropped the Colt and followed Slattery, backstepping into the jail and still holding Harold.

Slattery shoved Harold away from him and slammed the door shut behind Elmer. Harold dropped to his knees, gripping his leg with both hands. Elmer stood flat-footed, watching Slattery and Wright and

Doctor Hobson fire through the smashed glass of the window.

'That's enough,' Slattery said. 'They aren't shooting over there! They don't want to hit their brothers!'

The fusillade stopped. Powder smoke drifted on the air of the office, its smell overpowering. Wright leaned his back against the stone wall, his weight off his wounded leg. He wiped the sweat from his forehead.

Slattery looked at him. 'You crazy?' he said. 'Firing from that window. They could've picked you off.'

Wright shook his head. 'I hadn't watched from the window, you would've crossed to the hotel.' He nodded to his own words. 'If I hadn't been able to see the shadows of them waitin' to pick you off from behind Rinehart, you'd've been killed.'

CHAPTER SEVENTEEN

'I could've been killed!' Irving Rinehart cried. He'd crawled past the lobby door, sprawled flat on the splinters of glass that littered the floor, his body shaking. 'Openin' up that way! If I hadn't dropped out there, I'd've been killed!'

'Shut up!' Nathan Elkins snapped.

'But I was standin' in the open! They started shootin' and you . . .'

'Shut your mouth!' Clay Leonard, crouched alongside the bullet-shattered window, swung the Spencer rifle and smashed the iron barrel down onto the hotelman's lower left arm. Rinehart bellowed in pain. 'You broke it! Oh, you broke it!' He began to crawl sideways to escape another blow. Clay took off his hat. He edged his face higher and higher until he could chance a look across the street.

There was no movement inside the jail, nothing he could see clearly. Dammit! Damn the one who'd opened up from the jail! He'd given Slattery his chance to hit Harold and then use him for cover! They had four of their family locked in their cells, Cletus and Elmer, two of his cousins. Firing through the jail door and window was out. Ricocheting bullets could kill anyone inside, his own included. The building's stone walls were two feet thick. There was no way to reach the place.

Rinehart had reached Byron Kenneally

and the husband and wife hotel guests who had taken cover behind the lobby registration desk. The Winstons huddled together so terrified neither was able to talk or move. The hotelman groaned and moaned while Kenneally took hold of his shoulder to help him sit.

'My arm,' Rinehart whimpered. 'It's broken. He broke it.'

'You, Fat Man,' Clay snapped. 'Get back here.'

'My arm—'

Clay left Nathan crouched at the window and crawled across the floor. He raised the Spencer as though he intended to swing it again.

Rinehart cowered, gripped the broken forearm. 'Please, I can't do anything.'

'Get on your feet,' Clay ordered, 'and go across to the jail.'

'M'arm. I can't walk.'

'On your feet, I said.' He saw Kenneally's mouth open to speak, and he motioned with the Spencer for Kenneally and the Winstons to stay quiet. 'Slattery's got four of our kin inside the jail,' he added quickly to Rinehart. 'We have four of you. Tell him we'll make an even trade. Four for four.'

'He won't agree.'

'You tell him. Four for four. And we want a second wagon. We'll hold our hostages until we're out of this valley. The doctor comes, too, along with Cletus.'

'But he won't—' The raised rifle barrel again threatened. Rinehart gripped his arm tighter and pushed his heavy weight onto his knees. He looked at the other two men prisoners, and the woman. 'One of them can go.'

'I want you, Fat Man. I want the money that's in that bank. Ten thousand, I want. Tell Slattery he has thirty minutes, or I'll shoot the woman first and throw her out in the middle of the street!'

*　　　*　　　*

'The door's openin',' Al Wright said. He leaned his shoulder against the window frame, the carbine held barrel-down as a crutch to support his wounded leg. 'It's Irv Rinehart. He's comin' over here.'

'Don't show yourself,' Slattery warned. 'Let him come all the way across.'

But the hotelman did not walk to the jail. He halted in mid-road and called, 'Slattery! Tom Slattery!'

Slattery kept his body behind the window frame. 'Keep walking, Irving. We'll cover you.'

'Slattery, listen!' Rinehart yelled the words loud enough to be heard in the buildings, on both sides of Centre. 'They're holdin' me prisoner! Me and Byron Kenneally and a man and a woman! Listen! They want to trade us for the four prisoners you have in the cells! They'll kill us if you don't trade!'

'Keep walking,' Slattery repeated. 'Come in here.'

'No, Slattery! Don't you understand!' He gripped his left arm with his right hand and painfully raised the wrist. 'They've broken my arm! They'll shoot us! The woman first, if you don't get them another wagon and free those prisoners!' His voice rose higher, pleading. 'They want ten thousand from the bank, and the doctor to go with them, and time to ride out of the valley!'

'I can't agree to that.'

'You have a half hour! Tom, do what they say!'

Slattery edged out his head carefully, until he could see Rinehart, and the door and windows of the hotel. 'Come in here,

Irv. You can make it.'

Rinehart shook his head. 'They've got their guns on me! I have to go back! Don't let them kill us!'

He looked helpless, pathetic, standing alone in the road holding the arm and trying to control his agony. He glanced up and down the street, from one end of the town to the other. His words were meant for every man, woman, and child in the town.

'Don't let them murder us! Please! Please!'

And he turned and walked quickly back toward his hotel.

★   ★   ★

'What will we do?' Doctor Hobson questioned.

'You fix m' leg,' Harold Elkins said. 'We're gonna be in a wagon. I want it bandaged.'

'Yes, dammit,' his brother Buster called from the rear of the jail. 'Only a half hour, Doc. Better work fast, and check Cletus.' He stood at the front of his cell, pressed eagerly against the iron bars of the door. He stared down at the wounded men, making it clear what he thought, that Clay and Nathan had taken care of everything through the hotelman, and they would be let out right away, and it didn't matter now if it was known Cletus was his kin. 'You both move!'

'We'll carry Cletus out,' Elmer said. 'Jest you come 'long with us, Doc.'

Harold limped into the cell where his cousin lay and sat alongside the bunk. Blood showed between his fingers that gripped his wound. He was in pain, but in spite of this the same confidence shown by Buster and Elmer filled his face, his eyes shining with it.

'We can't do much else,' Al Wright said to Slattery. 'I'll go along with you on any trade.'

Slattery had not moved. Rinehart was inside the hotel again, and Slattery could not make out a movement through the lobby window. The wagon headed in from the east end had turned off at Four Corners. The walks and porches were deserted, each door and window shut and locked, the buildings and the alleyways as uncannily silent as the street.

'We have to decide,' Wright said. 'Tom?'

Slattery continued to watch the street.

Yellowstone City was a tight-built town. Each store that had been erected had been planned in a straight line out from the first structures which faced Four Corners. Men or wagons, anyone or anything leaving town could be watched and covered from half a hundred spots. Men hidden, with guns ready, could cut off the Elkins and Leonards easy enough. But hostages could be killed in the first burst of gunfire. He couldn't control that, any more than he could control the increase of cold sweat across his shoulders, down his back, under his arms.

He looked around at the doctor. 'Hurry with the leg, Doc.'

'You damnwell better!' Buster Elkins snapped. He watched Slattery, the ugly glare in his eyes showing he planned for some future time, when things would be different for him and Slattery.

Doctor Hobson glanced up from Harold's wound. 'I'll go with them.' He nodded at Cletus, who still breathed but seemed smaller and paler 'He'll need me.'

'You better,' Elmer said. He stood near the bunk, his eyes on his younger brother. 'He dies, there'll be five of you with us.'

Slattery turned, knowing the truth of the
181

threat, wanting to slash out with the carbine and smash the gunman's face. His own face was haggard, his nerves jumpy, his own fears alive in him, knowing the others held with Rinehart had the same need to live. He took one step toward Elmer, not actually sure what he would do.

The knocks on the jail's rear door stopped him.

Slattery moved fast. One of his hands motioned for Al Wright to keep clear of the door before Slattery passed close to Buster Elkins' cell and stopped with his body tight against the thick timber of the door frame.

'Who is it?'

'Barney Akkesson. Open up, Tom.'

Slattery slid back the heavy iron bolt. He unlocked the door, then opened it wide enough for the chairman of the Town Council to rush inside.

'We heard Irv!' Akkesson said. 'Everyone in town knows!' His stare shifted from Slattery to Wright, then to the doctor and the men in the cell block. He added quietly, 'We're asking Phil Lashway to take the money from the bank.'

'There's no promise they'll let the hostages go,' Slattery told him.

'It's four people's lives,' Akkesson said.

'Five, with Doc going along. We have no other choice.'

Slattery shook his head. 'We still can't be certain.'

'Don't listen to that sonovabitch!' Buster Elkins snarled, cursing. 'That bastard'll get his soon . . .'

Slattery's swinging blow of the Winchester cut off the prisoner's words as the solid oak stock smashed into the center of Buster's chest and drove him staggering across the cell into the stone wall.

Harold's eyes bulged at the suddenness and viciousness of the blow. Elmer didn't move because Al Wright's quickly raised carbine was aimed at his head. Buster gagged to catch his breath, his expression a mixture of pain and horror. 'You're crazy! You are, you're crazy!'

Slattery made another threatening gesture with the Winchester. 'Not one more word,' he said low and cold. 'No matter what, none of you says one more word.'

Then, he nodded to Akkesson, his voice steely. 'Have them get the money and the wagon, so they can see it's being done from across the street. Get the town men behind cover with their guns. Into the alleys, on the roofs. I don't know, there just might be another way.'

CHAPTER EIGHTEEN

To Myron Blumberg the day was beautiful.

He had just spent the happiest night he could remember since he'd come to Montana Territory. Frank and Ellen Shields had welcomed him with open arms when he had driven out to their homestead last night. The evening with them, their young children, and Judy, had passed so quietly, playing guessing games, laughing and talking. The same happy, content talk and ease and laughter had been a part of the fine breakfast Ellen had prepared this morning. And now, Judy sitting alongside him on the wagon seat, the quiet calm way she had of being with a friend, her eyes closed while she rested from the long drive, made him remember the years he'd had so long ago. He remembered that time happily today, not sadly as he'd done so many, many times. It would be a good day. The future would be easier for him because of the night and this morning.

The valley was beautiful. The sun was already hot, the dry wind of summer sweeping across the high grass and making it ripple and sway like a golden-green sea closed in on all sides by the towering granite might of the mountains. The timber along the Calligan, full-leafed, blocked any view of Yellowstone City. Myron felt the same satisfaction about going in to open his store. His customers were his friends, like the Shields and Tom and Judy Slattery. He would work hard today, and that, too, would be good.

'We'll be at the bridge soon,' he said. 'Tom will really be surprised.'

Judy opened her eyes, smiling. 'He certainly will.' The blanket Frank Shields had tucked over her coat had kept her warm and comfortable. Her long black hair was bound at the nape of her neck with a bright blue ribbon. She was a beautiful woman to Myron, and he thought of the years ahead, when she and Tom and this child she carried and the other children the Slatterys would have, would come in and visit and spend time at his store.

The town became visible ahead, beyond the trees that had branched out to spread over the river and shade the bridge. The heavy delivery wagon's wheels rumbled across the thick logs. Then, they became almost silent again, churning up dust as they rolled onto the worn roadway leading into Centre.

Myron suddenly noticed the quiet: the buildings were closed, the town's main street, the walks, the porches, all empty and quiet. No horses were tied at the hitchrails. The single wagon in sight was the light wagon he knew was owned by Barney Akkesson. It had been drawn up at the head of the alley between the jail and the bank. No one tended it. The horse and wagon simply waited, alone in the empty street.

Judy leaned forward holding the blanket close around her. 'I thought everyone would be out,' she said.

'They should be.' Myron tightened his right hand on the reins to turn the wagon and cut down behind the buildings.

The door of the blacksmith's shop opened. Joe Bush stepped outside. He waved to Blumberg to drive toward him, but he did not shout or call.

Judy's face was worried. She stared at the sheriff's office. 'Tom?' she said. 'Myron, the jail window is broken!'

'It'll be all right,' Myron told her. 'Just stay calm. It'll be all right.'

Shaking the reins, he moved his horse faster, and he leaned down from the seat to talk with Joe Bush the instant they reached him.

*   *   *

'What's happenin' there?'

Standing at the hotel lobby window, his body flat against the wall so he couldn't be seen from the jail, Clay Leonard had watched the delivery wagon roll across the bridge. He'd watched while the driver swung off the road towards the blacksmith's, and now he could see that a man hurried outside to meet the wagon. Clay motioned to Rinehart, waiting near the registration desk with the Winstons and Kenneally. 'Get over here, Fat Man.'

Rinehart moved as fast as he could. He'd found if he kept the broken arm pressed to his side, and gripped tightly, he felt less pain. He stopped alongside Leonard, the arm held away from the gunman. 'You're not sendin' me out again?'

Clay pointed westward. 'What are they doin' there?'

The fear in Rinehart's eyes changed, became guarded. Clay grabbed the hotelman's shoulder. 'He's takin' them off the road. Who's the woman?'

Rinehart's head began to shake. Clay gripped the shoulder tighter. He swung Rinehart around and held him as though he meant to hurl him against the wall. 'You think that arm's bad? I bounce you around, you'll know how bad it can hurt! Who is she?'

'Slattery.' Rinehart barely whispered the words. 'She's Tom Slattery's wife.'

Clay let go of Rinehart's coat. He stood for almost a full minute and stared along the road. He looked across at the jail. The men in the sheriff's office hadn't yet been able to see the wagon. If the blacksmith had let the horse travel another twenty feet, Slattery would know his wife was in town. But the black man hurried to get her off the street.

A small smile cracked the corners of Clay's mouth.

He shoved Rinehart toward the other hostages. He motioned for Nathan to move away from the opposite side of the window.

'Lock up after me, Nathan. One of them tries anythin'.' He spat out the word.

'Shoot!'

He went to the lobby's rear door and turned the key in the lock. Once outside he hesitated at the closed door only the fraction of a second it took for him to hear Nathan snap the lock shut inside. Lewis Elkins waited in the yard with the family's horses and the horse and wagon they had taken from the livery. Clay waved for his cousin to follow him. They both broke into a run, past the backsides of the buildings.

The black man hadn't taken the delivery wagon into his shop. He'd stopped the horse in the alleyway alongside the barn. The bony storekeeper and the black man were helping the Slattery woman step down from the front seat. Clay turned the corner into the alley and was on them so quickly the woman was frozen where she stood on the step plate. Neither man with her could act.

'She stays in the wagon,' Clay ordered.

Joe Bush turned toward him. Clay slammed the rifle barrel into the black man's chest, driving him backwards. Myron Blumberg kept hold of Judy Slattery. 'No, don't,' he began, 'she's...'

Clay's outstretched hands shoved the carbine hard into Judy's stomach. She cried out, but the gunman kept pushing. 'Stay on the wagon seat! Get up with her, both of you!'

The small storekeeper helped Judy sit. She was bent over, her body almost doubled under the blanket that had covered her legs. 'She's hurt!' Myron told Clay. 'You hurt her!'

'Drive into the street!' Clay snapped. The rifle muzzle centered on Joe Bush. 'Climb up with them!' And when Bush obeyed, 'Straight to the hotel!'

'But she's hurt—'

'Drive, storekeeper!' Clay snarled. 'Keep to the middle of the road! I want them to see you comin!'

Joe Bush's arms were around Judy. Her eyes were closed, her face pale, her breath heavy and labored. She leaned against Bush, not talking or opening her eyes while the wagon swung into the street.

Clay and Lewis walked alongside the big iron-rimmed front wheels. 'Stay behind cover with me,' Clay told his cousin. 'Soon as Slattery spots this, he'll show himself. Be ready to blow him out of the jail window.'

★　　★　　★

Clay took only two strides along mid-street before he spotted the men.

'Sonovabich!' he muttered, looking up at the roofs and false fronts of the buildings.

He'd had it made, he'd believed. He'd sent Rinehart across to the jail with his demands, and the hotelman had come back with word that Slattery had agreed. But what did he see now! Men with guns were on the roofs and behind the board false fronts. They waited in the alleys. Far out to the east a dust cloud showed many riders approached the town. They'd have more weapons to add to the lineup against them ... Well, dammit, he had the heavy wagon he'd wanted, not the flimsy light wagon that had been left between the jail and bank. He had Slattery's woman.

'That sonovabich,' he repeated aloud, snapping the words across his shoulder to his cousin. 'On the roofs, you see them?'

'I do. That bastard went back on his word.'

'He'll pay ... damn him ...' Clay raised the Spencer rifle. He held the muzzle pointed into the woman's face, warned, 'None of you moves 'til we reach the hotel.'

'She's hurt,' Joe Bush said. 'You hurt her with that rifle.'

191

'You shut, Negra. Be lucky I didn't leave you dead back there.' A slight motion centered the muzzle on Myron Blumberg. 'You, too. Stop where we'll be behind the wagon when we reach the porch.'

'She's carrying a baby,' Myron told him. 'Let her go.'

'To the porch.' The rifle barrel jabbed into the black man's side. Bush didn't flinch or release the hold he had around Judy.

'Keep goin',' Clay ordered. His eyes flicked from roof to roof, seeing more men, all watching and waiting. 'Keep goin' and do exactly what you're told.'

*　　　*　　　*

'Good Lord!' Al Wright muttered. He had been standing at the side of the window, not showing himself but feeling the good warmth of the sun that came in through the broken glass. He could smell hot coffee and frying bacon, and he'd realized he hadn't eaten, that he was very hungry, and Irving Rinehart hadn't had their breakfast sent over.

That was the moment he'd seen Myron's wagon and had muttered to himself. He tried not to be anxious or nervous. 'Tom,' he said. 'Come here.'

Slattery left the cell where he'd been helping the doctor. He sidled up to the window, keeping his body behind cover.

There was a moment of silence while he stared outside.

Surprise, then shock swept across his face. As suddenly, fear, and anger. Judy ... He had felt so much fear of being hurt or killed himself, because of Judy and the baby, and now this. She looked sick, bent forward on the seat, held by a very worried Joe Bush. Myron stared across at the jail, his lost, fearful worry as pronounced as Joe's.

Slattery edged his head out carefully. He couldn't shoot. The two men who used the wagon for cover held their weapons on Judy and the men with her. He couldn't yell or threaten.

Clay Leonard did the yelling. 'Slattery! Slattery, tell them on the roofs and in the alleys to hold their fire! You want her alive! Them alive?'

'They won't fire.' He judged the distance into the wide-open roadway where the sand was the color of copper under the driving hot sun. He could never reach Judy.

Nobody could reach her. 'Don't hurt her, Leonard.'

The wagon stopped. On the porch the lobby door swung open. A rifle barrel jutted out, aimed at the wagon seat.

Clay's head appeared above the horse's rump. His eyes switched from the jail to the bank. His face was strained between hate and satisfaction. To Slattery the stretch of open brownish earth between Clay and the jail looked like a thousand miles to cross. Slattery did not move. He watched Joe Bush begin to edge his big body onto the step plate, his arms outstretched to support Judy.

'She all right?' Slattery called. 'Joe? My?'

'She's goin' in with us!' Clay snapped back. 'We've got seven, Slattery! Seven to trade for our four and the money!'

'She all right, Myron? She looks sick!'

Blumberg half-turned but the barrel of the weapon in Clay's hands was jabbed into the small storekeeper's chest. Myron took hold of Judy's shoulder and eased her down to Joe Bush.

'If you've hurt her . . .' Slattery started.

'You don't threaten us!' Clay screamed the words. 'You want her, Slattery! Come out and make the trade! You sonovabich,

194

get them guns off the roofs and outa the alleys!'

Judy was on the ground. Joe Bush held one of her arms, Myron the other arm, helping her walk. She set one foot carefully in front of the other, as though she balanced herself on a tightrope.

Slattery watched his wife start up the stairs. She'd stumble and fall, he felt, if she wasn't helped.

He couldn't fire. Clay and Lewis Elkins reached the screen door first, their weapons aimed.

Slattery continued to watch even after the screen door swung in and closed behind Judy and the men. He stepped back and wiped the sweat from his forehead.

'Al,' he said. 'Call into the yard and have the men move out of the alleys and off the roofs.'

'They're willing to give the money, Tom.'

'Off the roofs,' Slattery repeated sharply. He turned toward the cells, his voice losing its sharpness, as though pleading.

'Doc, go over and see how she is.'

CHAPTER NINETEEN

Clay moved fast to the window as soon as he was inside the lobby. He stood behind the shattered glass, in plain view, his face flushed with the certainty he would not be shot. Not now, while he held Slattery's wife. He did everything for his kin to be sure he'd bring every man of his family back home to their women. His love for his brothers and cousins was part of his every breath, and he was sure the feelings of a man like Slattery were just as strong.

Scuffs of boots and shoes behind him didn't matter to Clay. The Slattery woman was being helped into the small hotel office. The others were so terrified they'd give no trouble.

Across the street the jail door opened.

Good, Clay thought. Now he'd get what he wanted! He waited for Slattery to come out first. Cletus would have to be carried. That's why he'd made certain the delivery wagon was left where it was.

But it wasn't Slattery who stepped through the doorway.

The doctor, holding his black medical

bag, crossed the walk and stepped down into the street to cross to the hotel.

'Go back!' Clay called. 'You stay with Cletus!'

The doctor did not slow his step.

'Back, I said!' Clay hunched forward with the rifle aimed. 'We don't need you!'

Doctor Hobson walked up onto the porch. He reached the door and opened it without looking at Clay. Clay raised his weapon as though he intended to force the doctor outside. 'Dammit, I told you we don't need you!'

'I'm here to examine Mrs. Slattery,' Hobson said, and he continued on through the lobby.

Clay cursed. He couldn't shoot the man who'd keep Cletus alive. His stare followed Hobson until he went into the office. Clay's hateful eyes swept across the faces of the hostages, the terrified old woman and her husband, Rinehart and Kenneally, the storekeeper, the blacksmith. They wouldn't try anything, not with Nathan and Lewis ready to shoot.

Clay cursed again. He stepped to the center of the window, then stood glancing up and down the street, at the roofs and the false fronts and alleyways. The riders to the east were more than a mile from the town. He couldn't see a sign of the men who waited with their guns. Slattery had had the word passed. He'd win, Clay thought. He'd made Slattery back down, despite the fact the doctor had come across . . .

Doctor Hobson appeared in the office doorway. 'She's bleeding,' he told Clay. 'I should take her to my office.'

'You take her nowhere. She stays here.'

'She's carrying a baby. She's hemorrhaging.'

'Go back over there!' Clay moved quickly to the registration desk, past the hostages, and into the office.

A blanket covered Judy Slattery. Clay didn't look at her. He sensed her weakness. That was enough. He closed the doctor's bag and handed it to Hobson.

'Tell Slattery she gets help when I get my brother!'

Hobson began to answer. His words were cut off when Clay shoved him out of the doorway.

The doctor tried to turn, but Clay kept shoving and pushing, holding the rifle in both hands, forcing him through the lobby.

'She needs me,' the doctor said. 'She'll bleed to death.'

'When I get my brother!'

'Me!' Rinehart interrupted. 'Let me go with him! He should fix my arm!'

Clay swung the rifle barrel at the hotelman. Rinehart ducked away, missed by a fraction of an inch. "You don't need me!' he cried. 'My arm's broke!'

'Let him go,' Byron Kenneally said. 'He's hurt. You don't need him.'

Lewis Elkins had opened the front door. Clay forced the doctor out onto the porch and slammed the door behind him.

'Tell Slattery!' Clay warned wildly. 'He trades!'

Hobson went off the porch.

Clay watched him until he was in mid-street. Then he again stepped to the window.

'You don't need Mr. Rinehart,' Byron Kenneally repeated. 'You have enough of us. Let him go!'

Hobson had reached the jail. The door was opened for him. Clay turned on his bootheels. The hate and anger were still in his eyes, yet his lips cracked in a knowing, disgusted smile.

'You stupid bastard,' he said to Kenneally, 'willin' to stand for him.' He saw the shock spread across Rinehart's face, how the hotelman began to back away. 'I'll tell you how he set you up. Every last bit of the plan he had to beat you out of your election.'

Slattery listened while Doctor Hobson told him about Judy. His nerves jumped, sent alternating waves of cold and warmth through him, his edginess getting jumpier and jumpier with each word of how badly hurt she actually was.

'. . . so I'm not certain how much she is bleeding,' Hobson finished, 'but she can't stay over there.'

Slattery's face showed nothing, no fear, no worry, no anger, none of the feelings which sliced through him, cutting like a knife into his brain and heart. He picked up his carbine and went to the window. The sun's heat hit him a sledgehammer blow. His eyes squinted against the glare off the copper-colored sand. He could see Clay Leonard directly across from him in the hotel window. The gunman stared as intently at him.

Clay wouldn't shoot, not right this minute, Slattery was sure. Clay had him on his knees. That's what the bastardly killer thought. It had all been so easy, the decisions, despite the worry and fear, as long as he wasn't caught in the terror of the hostages, as long as decisions could be made and the ones you loved didn't have to pay . . .

Slattery whirled around on his bootheels.

'Let them out of the cells,' he said to Al Wright.

The lawman simply looked at Slattery, his lips parted.

Slattery saw the grin on Buster Elkins' face, how his brother Harold and cousin Elmer straightened and grinned and stepped toward the cell doors.

'Let them out,' Slattery repeated harshly.

His sidelong glance at Wright made the lawman move, using his carbine as his crutch, his confusion still in his expression while he took the cell keys from the rack.

Slattery walked to the desk. 'You'll carry your brother on the bunk mattress,' he told Elmer. 'You and Harold and Buster.'

Buster laughed. 'You heard him, Deputy. Let us out.'

'No!' Slattery snapped in an oddly quiet voice. 'You're not being let out! You're being taken out!'

While Buster stared at Slattery, and Elmer and Harold stared, their grins suddenly wiped from their faces, Slattery pulled open the desk's top drawer. He took a box of shotgun shells and tore off the cover. Methodically, as though every thought he had, every motion he made, was definite and fully decided, he stuffed the entire boxful of shotgun shells into his pockets. He threw the empty box onto the floor.

Buster, Harold, and Elmer gave careful glances at Slattery, the three directed by Al Wright as they bent over to lift the mattress which held Cletus.

Wright led them out of the cell block, his carbine in his hands.

Before they reached the desk, Slattery turned to the gunrack and lifted a Greener shotgun from its place. He handed the Winchester to Hobson. 'It has a full load,' he told the doctor. He broke the shotgun, checked the two No. 10 shells in the chambers. He took a .44 Colt from its place, checked the cartridges in the drum, and jammed the weapon down under his belt buckle.

'Stay behind me, Doc,' he told Hobson. And to Wright, 'Hold them at the door.'

Slattery laid the Greener on the desk top and reached up and grabbed one of the coiled lariats off a wall hook. He made a loop and walked to Buster. 'You've got the big mouth!' he said in the same oddly quiet, low, cold voice. 'Open it!'

Buster obeyed. Slattery brought the coil down over Buster's head, roughly, placing the rope into the open mouth. As roughly he tightened the noose. Buster gagged, took a firmer grip on the mattress while Slattery whipped more coils of rope through the air and threw turns around Harold's, then Elmer's neck.

Slattery tightened the rope until each man had to strain to breathe. Then he again picked up the Greener shotgun.

'Walk slow!' He said. 'One bad move, I'll snap your necks like I would a snake! Start out!'

The three were frozen in terror. Half-choking, eyes staring wide, Buster walking backwards, the other two on the opposite end of the mattress, they moved into the street.

*   *   *

'That sonovabitch!' Clay Leonard snarled. 'Nathan!'

Nathan left Lewis with the hostages and

hurried to the window. An obscene curse spit from his lips.

Clay repeated the curses.

Buster, Elmer, and Harold barely reached mid-road carrying Cletus on the mattress stretcher before Slattery, holding the lariat, and the shotgun on them, ordered them to set Cletus down in the street. There wasn't a chance of shooting Slattery or the gimp-legged sheriff, both of them safe behind Elmer and his cousins.

'He can kill them,' Nathan blurted. 'They can't move!'

'You bastard!' Clay yelled. 'Slattery, we made a deal! You wanted a trade!'

'No! You wanted the trade!' Slattery yelled as loudly. 'You let go of the people you have, now!' He jerked the rope, making his prisoners straighten and gasp to catch their breath. 'Or they can die right in front of you!'

★　　★　　★

Slattery's answer, its wildness, savageness, echoed from the street into the alleys, up over the false fronts and roofs to die somewhere out in the silence of the river timber and along the broad grassy plain.

He'd lost, he believed, if Judy died. He'd failed to act before, to give the terrorists back exactly what they gave. He paid, through Judy. He was paying this very instant, with Judy bleeding, her life in the balance, her lifeblood giving the gunmen their edge while the sun drove down on him and he smelled the animal smell of the horses that waited hitched to their wagons, a smell which had been always clean and fine and good to him, but now pressed in on him like the burning heat and fear and terror . . .

'Get in a line, the three of you!' Slattery ordered.

He jerked on the rope, and the three coughed and gagged and crowded together in front of the mattress.

'Send them out!' Slattery shouted. 'Leonard, Elkins, send them all out!'

He took the rope in the hand that held the shotgun and leaned down over Cletus Leonard. He pulled once at the bandage across the unconscious man's wound, loosening the cloth. His second pull ripped the entire bandage away.

Blood was bright crimson across Cletus' chest, down his side. Slattery heard the doctor's, 'No, you can't!' and Wright's gasp of shock as he raised the bloody bandage higher for it to be seen from inside the hotel.

'You let her die,' he yelled, 'he'll die!'

Slattery's arm swung aside and blocked the doctor to keep him from going to Cletus.

'You don't help him, Doc! You come with me!'

Clay answered with a vicious curse. The clopping of horses' hoofs was loud to the east. Wright's voice was close and loud. 'Tom, it isn't right!' Slattery snapped across his shoulder, 'Follow me, dammit! Back me!'

He hurled the bandage down into the dust of the street, again grabbed the rope, tightening on it, while the twin barrels of the Greener jabbed the spines of his three prisoners. 'Walk to the hotel! Doc, stay with us!'

Clay's cursing stopped. Shadows made quick motions behind the shattered lobby window. The three stepped carefully, forced ahead. Out of the corner of his eye Slattery caught more movement. The riders who'd come in from the east were Byron Kenneally's men. They had reached the far side of Four Corners, had been told by the shouts of the town men what had happened, and they continued ahead through the intersection, horse pressed to horse, filling the road from walk to walk, each man, twenty to thirty of them, with revolver, rifle, carbine or shotgun in hand, prepared to fight.

Elmer, Buster, and Harold reached the bottom porch step. The screen door flew open and Rinehart came stumbling out. The momentum of the push he'd been given from inside took him to the porch edge. He caught himself. His heavy body teetered back and forth, as though he'd fall headlong down the stairs.

'He'll die!' Clay Leonard screamed from inside. 'One more step, I shoot him! Slattery! Let them go!'

'Please! Please!' Rinehart pleaded. Tears streamed over his cheeks, wet his fat jowls. 'Please, Slattery!'

'You'll lose Elmer first!' Slattery called. The twin barrels pressed the nape of Elmer's head. 'Shoot, and it's your brother's life!'

'Clay, he's crazy!' Elmer pleaded. 'I didn't kill no one! I won't hang!'

'We're comin' in!' Slattery tightened on the rope, jabbed with the shotgun, and passed the blubbering, crying Rinehart, on his hands and knees, crawling down the steps to reach safety behind Wright and the doctor.

★   ★   ★

Clay back-stepped, the Spencer rifle centered on the screen door.

'They're bein' forced in ahead of Slattery!' Nathan said. He motioned for Lewis to go toward the rear of the lobby, and he retreated with his cousin. 'Slattery'll shoot! He will!'

Almost to the second floor staircase, Clay snapped a glance across his shoulder at the hostages. All were huddled together, Kenneally and the Winstons crouched down behind the registration desk, the blacksmith and storekeeper crouched in the small office doorway. No time to get the woman and use her, no chance without a fight. He'd have to shoot the two men. Cletus would die. Elmer would die after his first shot, his head blown off.

His brother and cousins were at the screen door, their bodies blotting out the shine of the sun. One of them took hold of the knob and started to pull the door outward.

'They didn't kill anyone!' Nathan said. 'Clay, the doctor can still save Clete!'

Clay hesitated, looked at the hostages. Their faces were the faces of the dead, as helpless as Cletus bleeding in the street.

Clay backed another step. Nathan, beside him, glanced at Lewis to be sure he waited at the rear door.

The screen door opened. Harold and Buster crowded together to enter ahead of Elmer. Their mouths were open, their efforts to breathe bulging their eyes into the same pleading kind of stare Rinehart had had when he'd thrown the hotelman outside.

'We're goin'!' Nathan said. 'They won't hang! We fight, he'll kill them! We can reach the horses!'

Clay heard Lewis snap the key in the lobby's rear door. He glanced once again at the hostages, toward his brothers and cousins. He cursed Slattery. Everything had been to save his kin, not this, not seeing them die, not being the cause of their dying . . .

Clay backed to the open doorway. He kept backing, and slammed the door shut before he ran after Lewis and Nathan, following them to the yard to get their horses.

★　　★　　★

Slattery jerked hard on the rope and pulled the three prisoners off balance before he threw the lariat behind him for Wright to catch.

The doctor rushed past Slattery, around the desk, into the office. 'Myron, bring hot water, and bandages and blankets. I'll need them.' And to Bush, 'That man in the street. Stop his bleeding and take him over to my house.'

The Winston woman wept. Held by her husband, she did not make a sound, her sobs calming against his chest. Byron Kenneally waited alongside them. He looked toward the hotel porch and the faces of his men who stared in through the shattered window and screen door.

'Out back!' Kenneally told them. 'They're making a run for it! Go after them!'

Slattery walked past him and the man and wife. He stopped in the office doorway.

Doctor Hobson knelt over Judy. His body blocked what he did, but Slattery

210

could see her face. She was unconscious, her skin as pale and sallow as Cletus Leonard's, her mouth as lifeless and slack. He could not tell if she still breathed.

'Thank you,' Byron Kenneally's voice said behind him. 'Tom, we want to thank you.'

Slattery set the Greener down on the desk top and looked across his shoulder. He nodded to the Winstons, then said to Kenneally, 'Boys' tricks. They can lead to so much.'

Kenneally shook his head. 'It was all a plan, Tom. Rinehart . . .'

'He'll pay. But you don't spit in a man's face. No one does.'

Gunfire broke out somewhere behind the town, a single shot, followed by two more, the sounds muffled inside the walls of the building. Then other weapons cracked. The gunfight lasted barely a minute before the noises faded, gradually, to silence.

Al Wright had removed the rope from the three prisoners. Elmer Leonard, Harold and Buster Elkins, each man gasping to regain his breath, all stared at the rear door, as though they expected the gunfire to continue.

'They'll get them,' Kenneally said.

'There's only so far they can run.'

Slattery's head was bent, staring, listening to catch the slightest sign his wife breathed. The thought of adding words to Kenneally about the real reasons why the trouble had started went through his mind, what had gone wrong, how and why. But he did not speak. Right now, he did not feel like talk. Words were of no value.

He straightened in the doorway and watched the doctor.

He could only stand, and be near, and wait.

Photoset, printed and bound in Great Britain by REDWOOD BURN LIMITED, Trowbridge, Wiltshire